# CRUISIN' WITH VENGEANCE

### ROOSEVELT MOMPREMIER

iUniverse, Inc.
New York   Bloomington

# Cruisin' With Vengeance

*iUniverse books may be ordered through booksellers or by contacting:*

*iUniverse*
*1663 Liberty Drive*
*Bloomington, IN 47403*
*www.iuniverse.com*
*1-800-Authors (1-800-288-4677)*

*Because of the dynamic nature of the Internet, any Web addresses or links contained in this book may have changed since publication and may no longer be valid. The views expressed in this work are solely those of the author and do not necessarily reflect the views of the publisher, and the publisher hereby disclaims any responsibility for them.*

*ISBN: 978-1-4502-2786-5 (sc)*
*ISBN: 978-1-4502-2784-1 (dj)*
*ISBN: 978-1-4502-2783-4 (ebook)*

*Library of Congress Control Number: 2010906297*

*Printed in the United States of America*

*iUniverse rev. date: 06/02/2010*

# ACKNOWLEDGMENTS

I WANT TO ACKNOWLEDGE Joanne Mompremier, my wife of fourteen years, who was with me on a cruise ship as we talked about a fictional crime that would take place on the same ship. *Cruisin' With Vengeance* is my second book, but it won't be my last.

Dawson Baker has always been supportive of my efforts. He is just like a dad to me. We met many years ago on a cruise ship, and he could sense the future in writing I had in me. In 1996, he published my first book, *Cruisin' With the Dreamers.*

Angie Shumaker, a good friend, read the original *Cruisin' With Vengeance*, and she honestly exclaimed that there wasn't a person in the book she could like. So, I set out to revise my novel and give it a moral anyone could see.

Michael Lee Madsen, Sr., has creative overload and shows worldwide concern. He effectively throws all his innate ingredients together with his expressive compassion for the written word. Not only did he help me adapt my original book to an excellent screenplay, but he also helped me fine-tune the latest version of this book.

Donna Wauhob was a gem of a literary agent, the only one in Nevada at the time. She brought Mike and me together and forged a writing team that took good and made it better. Her positive attitude made it easy for me to develop and enhance my own literary ambitions. She died in 2008, and the world is a sadder place.

# CHAPTER 1

*Spring 1994*

AT EIGHT THIRTY FRIDAY morning, twenty-nine-year-old Rick Solomon was dismissed from the Miami Federal Correctional Institution, a pent-up rage within him. A rage that scorched his firm body from head to toe. What he felt was no ordinary hate or anger. It was something much deeper, much darker than even he could understand. He'd just done time for a crime he didn't commit, and he was filled with such a burning lust for revenge, he could barely contain it. He was five feet eight inches tall and weighed one hundred sixty pounds, most of which was pure muscle. He had brown hair, brown eyes, a round face, and an easy smile. As he walked out of his cell, Mosby, a neighboring inmate shouted, "Hey! Another innocent man is escaping." Laughter erupted from the nearby cells.

Rick went solid, and his muscles stretched as his cold look hid his desire to cripple Mosby for life. "You wouldn't have said that if I wasn't getting out!"

Mosby opened his mouth to smile with a mishmash of gnarled yellow teeth. "Bye, sweet meat. I'll miss you."

The guard broke up the moment. "Shut up, Mosby. I'll bring you back fresh meat that's not so tough."

The other prisoners continued to laugh. Rick looked at the guard, and his fists started flexing again, wanting to hit him just one time for old time's sake. "You wouldn't have said that either."

The guard barked back, "Hey! Get your stuff. They don't let you out of prison every day."

The guard looked into the cell. A series of hand-drawn caricatures of women with various parts of their torsos missing were sketched no higher above Rick's bed, no higher than if he had drawn them when he was lying

1

down. During his years in prison, Rick Solomon did not dream. He drew. Several of the bodies drawn on the wall looked like Rick had jabbed them many times with something sharp.

"What about your girlfriends on the ceiling?" the guard asked.

Three newspaper clippings of three women were taped to the ceiling. A faded headline alongside the pictures read, Justice Is Served. The clippings also had multiple jab marks.

Rick was impatient. "Keep the bitches. They've already given me enough wet dreams."

Rick left the prison and stepped onto the pavement. He was on the verge of tearing himself in two. His rage had built to such a high peak, he could actually feel the green dragon rise up. *I'm going to find the female scum and her friends and exact my pound of flesh.* But he suppressed the urge and fled because if he thought once more about the beatings and the vile degradation he'd suffered in prison, he was afraid that his anger might grow beyond containment and hysteria of a sort might grip him.

Now he realized that the clause in the Pledge of Allegiance that mentioned "and liberty and justice for all" was sheer nonsense and hogwash. If he had been falsely locked up for a crime he didn't commit, it meant the judicial system in America was undeniably wrong. In order for justice to be served, you couldn't rely on authorities. They were too damn slow, some too racist, and had too much paperwork to begin with. You had to make it personal, take justice into your own hands, bypass the screwed-up system entirely, and become an outlaw and punish harshly. You had to harshly punish any scumbag who trespassed against you.

Rick Solomon hailed a cab and pooled his money. The cab driver said, "Where to?"

"I have ninety-six dollars and twenty-seven cents to get me to 61 West Thirteenth Street," Rick said. His voice was deep and disturbed.

"That's Hialeah, right?"

"If that's not enough, then let me out."

The cab driver started the engine and pulled away from the curb. He gazed at Rick through the rearview mirror and shook his head like Rick was crazy. The Haitian cabbie was in his fifties. The ID over his visor revealed his name: Eric Dupuis. "Everything's cool, man," Eric said in French Creole-accented English. "Everyone needs a second chance."

Rick felt like his character had been assassinated without cause. He wondered if the cabbie viewed him as a felon with a list of heinous crimes on his rap sheet. Now he was mad as hell. He said, "I'm not a criminal. Yet. And what do you know about second chances?"

At a red light on 152nd Street, Eric swung around. Rick noticed he was wearing a cross necklace. It looked to Rick like it was almost identical to the one he used to wear as a kid. To Rick, a cross necklace was a symbol of peace, strength, and harmony.

Eric said, "I apologize if you thought I was insinuating. No disrespect. Your trip is approximately twenty-two miles. Figure it would run you about fifty bucks, sir. As for second chances, I have been there. I, too, have been given a second chance. And not a day goes by I don't thank God to bless the United States of America."

An awkward moment was born between them. Almost a mile later, Rick felt some sort of connection with the cabbie. He said, "Didn't mean to jump down your throat back there, bro."

Eric was cool as a cat. Typical islander. "No harm done. It's all good, my brother. It's quite all right."

Rick relaxed. "Your point is well taken."

They drove silently on Highway 874. As they merged onto the 826 freeway, Eric said, "Another time, another place."

Rick wasn't quite sure what he was leading up to; he played along. "How so?"

"Well, here you get food, drinks, a bed to sleep in, and you even get paid, however little the pay may be. Back where I'm from ..."

Rick waited.

Eric continued speaking. "They'd even force convicts to eat their own stool and drink their own pee."

Shocked, Rick wondered if Eric spoke the truth. But when he met his eyes through the rearview mirror, Rick was convinced he was for real. "This happened to you?" Rick asked.

Eric hesitated, let out a sigh, and then launched into a revelation: "The year was 1979. It seemed as though the world had turned its back on us. We had one political party. You either supported Baby Doc with the Tonton Macoutes or you were dead."

Rick pinched the bridge of his nose as Eric recounted his life story. "And then one night, I found myself living a nightmare when four soldiers whisked me away from my home and brought me downtown for questioning. They said I was a member of an organization planning to overthrow Baby Doc."

"Were you?"

"No. Never."

Rick thought pensively about the bizarre encounter. "Couldn't you prove your innocence?"

"There was no trial. Trials were for the civilized world. I was thrown in prison to die. And what I had to put up with was more gruesome than you can imagine. Certainly worse than you want to know."

For a moment, Rick wondered about the man's plight and why life had to be so cruel sometimes. "How did you survive?"

Eric's voice shook. "Faith. Hope. Courage. Nothing is impossible, you know? They had my body, true, but they couldn't take my spirit."

Rick blinked twice, disbelieving what he was hearing. "When did you come here?"

"Seven years ago. When they released me, my immediate family was already killed. With the help of friends, I boarded a crowded boat out of La Tortue bound for Miami. After eighteen days at sea with no food and hardly anything to drink, the coast guard picked us up. I barely made it. I knew the trip was dangerous," added Eric, "but I was willing to die to be free."

As they drove on the 826 freeway, Rick thought about the depth of the statement. Although he wasn't afraid of death, he, too, was going to need luck, faith, and hope. Finding one and not the others would bring him no relief from his pain. No relief from his nightmares. No relief from the embarrassment. No sense of victory.

They drove east on 934, off on Red, and zoomed up Thirteenth Street.

Rick said, "Must be tough for you to let go, uh?"

Eric smiled and said an emotional, heartfelt, "Oh, I did let go. In the beginning it wasn't easy. But as you get older, you learn to forgive your enemy. Because if you don't ..."

The cabbie shook his head as he pulled the Crown Victoria toward the driveway. Now face-to-face with Rick, he said, "Hell, never mind, young man. You'll have to figure that out on your own."

Rick was home. The house had not changed. It was a charming duplex with decoratively carved shutters, bars on the windows, scalloped fascia, wisteria creeping here and there, and sweetheart roses twined around the front porch. A six-foot statue of the Virgin Mary holding Jesus watched over the gate. Rick ran up to the doorstep and rang the bell. When the inner door swung open, he was greeted by Granny's barking dog. Granny squinted out through the screen door, smiled, and then unlocked the door.

"Oh, Rick, you're free. Thank you, Jesus," praised Granny, her face flushed with excitement.

Rick managed a smile as he embraced her. "Didn't you know that I was getting out today?"

Granny stepped aside to usher him in. "Yes, I knew," she admitted. "Gus and I briefly talked about your early release. But I didn't expect to be seeing you here so soon."

"Yeah, but with Gus's death and all, how can I stay away from you, Granny? After all, I'm the only one left. Oh, by the way, did he leave something here for me?" he said impatiently.

Granny smiled, indicating that she understood his impatience. The dog snapped at the air again in warning. "Cut it out." She allowed her tone to convey irritation. "Cut it out!" The dog sniffed her hand and retreated. Granny turned to Rick. "No. Nothing."

Rick's heart sank. "Are you sure about that?"

"I may be old, but my memory is sharp. So sharp that I even remember exactly what he said to me the last time he called."

A sprig of hope. "What did he say, Granny?"

"Come on outside," said Granny. "Let's have a chat."

Granny shuffled through the house, never entirely lifting either foot. Rick studied her, and he was captivated by what he saw. Her face was thin, wrinkled, and drawn with deeply carved lines at the corners of her eyes. The lines also framed her mouth. Her skin sagged. It was no longer as beautiful as shown in her wedding picture hanging on the wall. Since the last time he had seen her, she had lost more weight. Her gown hung loosely on her body.

Rick followed his grandmother across the carpet, through the kitchen, and out the back door. The backyard ran for at least fifteen feet before yielding to a garage with a built-in room. Granny sat down where she had been embroidering a tablecloth, which she did as a sort of second career. She had learned how to knit when she was in the Girl Scouts, and over the years she had parlayed her skills into a steady income. A cup of tea and the Bible sat nearby.

Granny groaned. Rick sat down beside her on a bench. "You all right, Granny?"

"I've had better days, my son."

Rick nodded, accepting that judgment. "I know."

"You know Gus died because he was a drug dealer," Granny said candidly. "Son, please don't—"

Rick pulled a face at her suggestive remark. "You know I care about him," he interrupted offensively. "But for now I need to know what he said."

For a second, Granny's eyes were hard. And the strings of wrinkles were pinched tightly around her mouth. "He said he was coming to see me. And then he calls back and says you will be out next week. And that Kim has a parcel for you." A solemn look appeared on her face. "That was the last time I ever spoke to him."

"Did Gus leave a number for her?"

"I don't know her, and I don't remember the number offhand—"

"Did you write it down, Granny?"

"My mind's not clear on a lot of things, especially numbers," she said, picking up on his bitterness while reaching for the Bible. "But yes, I did. In fact, I wrote it down in here."

Rick relaxed, offering her his brightest smile. "Good, Granny, very good."

"I told you I'm not that old."

"You're right," he conceded. "You're *not* that old."

"Do you have a place to stay?"

Rick stood and walked toward the outside entrance to the room. A cool breeze had risen, stirring the branches of the trees.

"I was hoping for my old room in the garage. You need a tenant?"

"Grandsons don't need to ask. I'll do anything for you."

"I learn to take nothing for granted, Grandma. Thanks."

He laid a sloppy kiss on her cheek and noticed a doll with braids in Haitian garb sitting next to her Bible. He picked up the doll, and had a wonderful flashback to his simple and peaceful life.

Four years earlier, Rick's grandmother sat in Rick's nicely decorated one-bedroom apartment. Two colorful fluff pillows adorned his bed. "This is a special doll from Haiti. It is meant to be given to those that you love," Rick said.

Granny smiled and said, "You didn't have to."

"There are lots of things in this world I don't have to do. But to give my Granny a present from my heart is something I want to do."

Rick recalled hugging his grandmother and saying, "Because it means I will always love you."

But now, four years later, sadness appeared on Granny's face. Rick noticed the sudden change and put the doll back down on the table. She said, "Rick my love, would you tell me again what happened to you on that boat?"

Rick's expression turned from cold to serious. "Granny, I'm not in the mood."

"I know it might hurt, but I just need to hear the truth once more, the truth I helped raise you and Gus to believe in."

"Only you and God know my truth."

Granny sat back in her chair. Rick took a deep breath and closed his eyes. And then he began to tell Granny his story: "It was a Sunday morning around 3:00 AM. I was going for a cup of coffee, and I saw that woman, Rachel, staggering about and ran to her assistance. She was drunk, probably drugged, and also bleeding all over. And the next thing I knew, she passed out. For a second, I was tempted to abandon her." Rick opened his eyes and raised a hand. He was looking right through Granny's eyes. "But as a gentleman—something that *you* taught me to be—I had to help."

Granny nodded understandingly, taking in every word. Her mouth open, closed, and open again like a fish in an aquarium tank. She had looked after her grandsons when their mother, a cocaine addict who couldn't care less, died from an overdose. The father, Jim Solomon, fit the same description. The boys were only two years apart. Rick was six and Gus was eight. She cherished them and treated them as if they were the focus of her life, until they were old enough and had been more or less dependent on each other for companionship and moral support. After earning their high school diplomas, their lives were on an oddly parallel course. Rick eked out a living at Eckerd photo lab and then landed a job on a cruise ship. On the other hand, Gus became a key figure in the international drug trade.

"I gave her mouth-to-mouth, and she started breathing again when this security guard appeared. He said, 'Let's get her to the infirmary.' I told him she was staggering through the hall. But he said he knew what happened."

Rick looked at his grandmother now with a serious expression. "I thought everything was all right, until Rachel screamed, 'I was raped!'"

Granny said, "But they knew you helped her."

"That didn't matter to them."

Rick paused, almost unable to go on. "I told the chief of security that I thought it was my duty to help Rachel. But he said that I was sneaking Rachel's violated body back to her cabin."

Granny interjected. "But that's not the truth."

"Granny, the truth was not what they wanted."

Rick's voice broke. He was almost on the verge of crying. But as a new man, he handled his grief well. "I begged them to believe that I had nothing to do with any of it. But they wouldn't buy it. Instead, I was told not to say anything more because I would have plenty of time to tell my story to the authorities."

Granny shook her head in disbelief. "Oh, Jesus." Her voice was barely above a whisper.

"And worst of all, Rachel's friends backed her up."

Granny said, "Did they ever launch an investigation to find the rapist?"

Rick blinked and drew in a deep breath. "They didn't need an investigation. They had me."

"I'm so sorry, my son. I've been praying day and—"

Rick suddenly remembered where he was at and interrupted her with a dry noise that sounded pure bitter when it came out. "Excuse me, Granny," he said, clenching his fists. "I need to call that girl."

Rachel Tolar cruised into the newest, hottest restaurant and club in South

Beach, Kaleidoscope, as if she owned the place. She was twenty-six years old and of medium height with exquisite features. Her short blonde hair glimmered like gold. Her face was captivating. Her nose was as pointed as an arrow. A nice suntan took work. And her riveting blue eyes were her greatest asset. As she moved through the crowded club toward the bar, heads turned. She attracted attention wherever she went. She was that much of a knockout.

"Hi, Sean," she said, greeting him with a mega smile and a twinkle in her eye. "What's happening?"

Sean Elmore, Rachel's favorite bartender, was a skinny, tall, good-looking gay black man who possessed an animal charm for men and women. His hair was curly black and greasy. He smiled and moved down the bar to join Rachel.

"Hel-lo, sweetie."

"Busy morning, isn't it?" Rachel said, displaying a row of perfect snow-white teeth.

He set a drink in front of her. "Typical Friday morning."

Rachel downed the drink in two great gulps. Sean said, "Boy, you were a thirsty one."

Rachel chuckled. "I needed the drink."

Sean was oblivious of the other patrons waiting for him to serve them. As far as he was concerned, the boss's girlfriend was his boss, too. "Wanna talk about it?"

"Derek wants to take me on another trip."

Sean's eyes went wide. "Another one?"

Rachel glanced over at a joker staring at her. Men could never resist Rachel's allure, her beauty, her stance, her poise, and everything else she possessed. "Yep. He wants us to bond."

"I can't wait to be rich."

Rachel laughed. "You're too honest."

Sean nodded in agreement and teased her, saying in a fake French accent, "Where this time? Paris, France?"

"Don't ask."

Sean refilled her glass. "That bad?"

"He wants to take me on a cruise this time."

"Oh, that's super, Rachel," he said with a dramatic tilt of his head.

"But I don't like cruises."

"I'm sorry, dear. But cruises are *sooo* romantic."

"To some maybe, but not to me."

Sean frowned. "So, you're not going?"

"I don't know."

"How does he feel?"

Rachel pulled on the drink more slowly this time. "He said he had already booked it."

Sean cocked his head like women do and said, "Derek *is* a gentleman. I'm sure he'll understand."

Rachel leaned closer, as if she was about to divulge a big secret. "Is he about?"

As much as she loved Derek, she didn't trust him any further than she could spit.

"I'm not sure, but the old man is."

"Is Derek being good?"

"Good as gold."

Sean looked away and then quickly gazed back at Rachel. "Look," he said, putting her mind at rest. "Don't you worry, sweetie. If Derek starts fooling around, you'll be the first one to know."

Rachel eased off the barstool, fished a hundred dollar bill from her purse, and handed it to Sean. "Thanks, Sean. Buy something nice for your main squeeze."

"I'll buy him a nose ring and pull him around. Where you off to?"

"I have a date with a psychic."

"You don't believe in that stuff, do you?"

"I do if she says nice things about me and Derek."

Rachel left the bar, and a short time later, she arrived at the psychic's place. The room was dark with heavy woven drapes. The smell of incense and candles permeated the air. A crystal ball and tarot card sat on a mantle. A nervous Rachel sat quietly in front of Alexis, who was in a trance. Another older woman sat nearby.

After a couple of minutes of silence, Alexis began speaking in tones of great authority. "You were born and raised in Harrisburg, Pennsylvania."

"How did you know that?"

The older lady raised a finger. "Shh!"

Alexis continued, "You lost your parents at a very young age. You moved to South Florida to stay with a cousin. You performed many jobs to make ends meet."

Rachel's head swam. What a difference five minutes made. As Rachel had driven over to Alexis's, she had been in total control of herself, rehearsing in her head how she would react during the session. "To get the best out of the reading," a friend had suggested, "you should relax and try to keep your mind blank. While sitting in the chair in front of Alexis, take a position and hold it. No extraneous body movements as the reading is given. And if Alexis pushes you to speak, say, 'maybe or I'm not sure.' Also, keep track of everything you said. The hits and misses, especially, because there's a tendency to be impressed by the hits in psychic readings and to ignore the misses." Now, as Rachel listened to Alexis, she felt like she was in less control.

"You went on many cruises," added Alexis. "They were fun, until the day you were raped."

Rachel struggled to stay calm and keep her mind blank at all times, and she did not give any verbal cues, just in case psychics could really read people's minds. She was determined to proceed with caution, trying to make it as tough as possible for Alexis, hoping that the reading would be wrong. But her efforts were indeed in vain. Instead, Alexis was now reading her like a book.

"And an innocent man was blamed."

While Alexis was silent for a moment, Rachel's thoughts turned back three years. Though the room was comfortably cool, Rachel felt warm and confused, as confused as she had been on board that ship. "How do you know all this?" she finally asked.

"There's a black aura around your body that can only be removed on another cruise."

Rachel's mind was racing. "But why would I need another cruise?"

With confidence, Alexis said, "Someone is planning your future, and you will bond with the sea."

Rachel closed her eyes and sighed in relief. "A marriage?" she whispered.

Alexis nodded, and whispered, too. "Yes. Definitely."

Rachel left the psychic's place feeling stunned. As she wheeled her Lexus onto Interstate 95, she grabbed her car phone and punched in Derek's number. Derek picked up on the first ring. "Derek here."

"It's me, honey, and I love you."

Derek Smalls. Twenty-six years old. He stood five feet ten inches tall with abundantly great looks. Long face, dimpled chin, short dark hair, and broad shoulders. His dazzling blue eyes were legendary. A real lady-killer. Derek laughed. "And will this be the same tomorrow?"

"That was yesterday and this is today," she said in a sexy, warm voice. "And I'm going on that cruise with you. Are you excited?"

Derek had a smooth way of talking. He said, "Sweetheart, I didn't mean for it to sound like that, but my money's safe. Good. So what changed your mind?"

She believed him. "Nothing special. Thought I should please you, darling."

After a short pause, Derek said, "This could get really good."

Rachel blushed, blew kisses into the phone, and pushed the End button. *Derek is going to get lucky tonight,* she thought.

# CHAPTER 2

DETECTIVE ROSS LEBLANC ENTERED his house. He put his jacket on a chair, and then he was knocked backward with a fist. Ross quickly regained his six-foot three-inch height and turned around to face his assailant, a tough-looking kid wearing jeans and a flannel shirt. The veins and muscles bulged at his neck, and his forearms seemed to radiate a chill that found its way into Ross's flesh. In the background, Ross could hear his seventeen-year-old daughter, Kim, screaming in extreme distress. Ross froze, too terrified to move.

"Freeze, asshole!" the intruder said, drawing his gun.

Ross ignored the warning. "All right, son. Put down the weapon."

"I'm not your fuckin' son. All I want you to do is get up slowly and face the motherfuckin' wall." His voice was deep, gravely, and malevolent, like something that belonged in hell. As Ross got up, the kid hammered him thunderously into the wall. Ross's teeth snapped together so forcefully that he would have bitten his tongue off if it had been in the way. He blinked, gasping. "What do you want from us?"

"Payback, motherfucker," he said, the pent-up violence still thick in his voice. "That's what I want."

Ross pleaded. "Payback for what?" He could smell the metallic odor of the blood running from the corner of his mouth.

Holding the gun to Ross's head, the kid said, "I want to know why you killed September, you punk. Was it for insurance money? Was it for fame? I want to know now."

Ross was sweating as if he was running a marathon.

"Listen, young man," Ross said plaintively. "I didn't kill my wife. It was an accident."

The kid grew more irritated. "Accident my ass. You plotted it all long. You dirty piece of shit. I want the truth. Now!"

"You can't handle—"

The kid didn't wait. "All right. No more farting around. On the count of three, you don't fess up, I will kill you both."

Ross was nearly paralyzed by fear. His heart was hammering so hard he didn't dare to flinch, in case it blew up.

"Three … Two … One!"

"Okay, okay," Ross said. "Put the gun down, and let me tell you what happened." But to his horror, the kid pulled the trigger.

Ross awoke nauseated. The kid was only a nightmare. Ross had a vivid mental picture of what might have happened if the dream was reality: his brains would have been found splattered all over the place, and Kim's body would probably have been mutilated. Lying in bed, he glanced at a picture of September, his late wife, who had died seven years earlier. The picture was the only artwork in the master bedroom. She was standing on a boat in sailing clothes with their daughter, Kim, who was only ten years old at the time. In the picture, Kim was blonde, fair, soft, beautiful, and shining with a very special innocence. Ross studied September's exotic features in the almost-real colors of Kodachrome, reflecting on the long years of solitude and grief.

Ross tried to place himself there, next to her. But when he couldn't, he reached out, grabbed the photograph. Pressing it against his chest, he willed time to turn back, wishing that their lives had turned out differently. The urgency of being with September grew so intense that at one point Ross could even feel and smell the soft texture of her skin.

"Don't leave me, please," he whispered, and his entire body shook. "I still love you."

Inevitably, no weight of passion could hold the memory of a lost one forever. September's soft skin scent retreated like an ascending balloon and was soon beyond his reach. Ross gave his head a vehement shake to clear his mind from his past, which never stopped haunting him. And then, in a fit of irrational fear, he put the picture down and ran to the basement stairs leading to Kim's bedroom. The room was empty. Ross's heart seemed to have swelled to the point of bursting. Then he caught a glance of the ornate digital Seiko clock. The time was thirty-five past eight. Only then did he realize that Kim had already gone to school and that it was Friday morning.

Ross Leblanc had been sixteen years on the force. Like most of his peers at the Miami Shores Police Department, he believed in justice and equality of human rights. Contrary to popular belief, he was doing a superb job keeping the bad guys off the streets—the ones who thought the law was just a sham to gull the ignorant masses into obedience. The city of Miami had become the number one murder city in the country, and he felt proud to be among the ones to protect, serve, and guard the safety of private citizens. That was why he became a cop.

That was why last month he was forced to shoot a twenty-two-year-old boy for allegedly raping a twelve-year-old girl. Ross hadn't planned on using his pistol for the arrest. The kid seemed so vibrant, so promising. But when he came along with the police squad to apprehend the boy, the creep opened fire on them, much to his disappointment. One officer was gut shot, rushed to Jackson Memorial Hospital, lost his spleen, developed a blood infection, and barely made it.

Ross Leblanc was almost six feet three inches tall. He weighted close to two hundred pounds, most of it muscle. He was, and had already been for many years, an active member of the Scandinavian fitness club. He had broad shoulders, crew-cut gray hair, shaggy eyebrows, and sharp, kindly brown and watchful eyes that missed nothing. In his midforties, Ross had an erect military bearing, an alert expression, and a politician's firm handshake.

From Kim's room he made his way up into the kitchen and grabbed a can of Sport Shake from the fridge. The cold shake hit his belly with a sensation. It tasted marvelous. Wonderful. Maybe it was just what he needed. Tossing the empty can in the waste disposal, he moved to the window, where he adjusted the curtains. The east side window provided a view of Biscayne Bay, where the morning sun cast a limpid shaft of light into the meadow. *What a beautiful day,* he thought.

Before going to work, Ross made his bed. The twenty-two-foot-wide master bedroom had a sitting area that included a chair and a stool, a dresser, and a corner desk. Above the desk was a shelf bearing a few books. Then he had breakfast: two slices of ham and a bagel with cream cheese, which he chased down with a glass of milk. When he was finished, he hand-washed the dishes and utensils and wiped off every bit of lint and dust around. All his life he had detested disorder, and he had a fetish for cleanliness. After taking a long shower, he dressed and headed for work.

Covering half a city block, the Miami Shores Police Department occupied an aging two-story building on One Hundredth Street NE and Second Avenue in Miami Shores. Reggie Sanders, the uniformed security guard, watched over the ungated entrance. As Ross pulled in, he waved at Reggie as usual and then slotted the Mustang in its designated parking space.

Reaching into the backseat, Ross grabbed his briefcase, double-checked his reflection in the rearview mirror just to make sure that he still looked sharp, opened the door, and walked to his office. Suddenly, it occurred to Ross that he was the only one around. He passed the many subdivided workstations and cramped offices. Still no one in sight. Not a living soul. Except for the crackling of the radios and walkie-talkies, the two-story building was full of Friday silence. It was very odd because even at this early hour, people were always on the move through the main lobby and hallways. He glanced at his watch. It was nearing nine. *Where is everybody?* he wondered.

When he also found Captain Cole's office empty, he smiled and suspected a game. As he approached, he could hear voices in his office from the corridor. He retraced his steps. "Definitely a game," he muttered. In his office, he found the entire Miami Shores Police Department morning staff. And they shouted in unison, "Good morning, Ross. How you feeling today?"

Shaking his head, Ross said, "I'm doing fine, thank you."

Captain Cole stepped forward. "Ross, we'd like to take this opportunity to congratulate you for doing a hell of a job here at this station for the past sixteen years."

Ross looked amazed. "Have I really been here for sixteen years?"

The staff laughed loudly.

"For this reason," continued Cole. "We're proud to offer you a package vacation for you and Kim aboard the biggest cruise ship in the world, the M/S *Redemption*. And you'll be going on Sunday!"

Cole, fifty-two years old, was six feet tall, utterly bald, with a white beard, brown eyes, long nose, and a beer gut. He wore brown dress slacks, white-and-brown checkered suspenders over a plain white shirt, and a yellow tie.

Ross said, "This Sunday! What if I had plans?"

The staff didn't listen to his argument. Someone shouted, "Spur of the moment!"

"This is the Memorial Day weekend, and the cruise will be jam-packed with single women," added Cole.

The staff laughed uproariously. Although Ross hated this awkwardness, he realized that he was probably the only single man among them. He was excited about the idea of the cruise.

"Guys, I appreciate the gesture," said Ross, trying to keep his excitement at bay. "But you all know how I feel about boats."

Cole said, "Don't give us that. You used to have one, remember? So, yes, you are going, and we all wish you a wonderful time. And I'd like to introduce you to your new partner from Los Angeles, Mr. Carl Levy."

There was scattered of applause.

Carl stepped forward and shook hands with Ross. He was tall and clean-cut, though he sported a ponytail. Dressed in white shirt, brown tie, and blue jeans, there was something peculiar about him that immediately captured

Ross's attention. And he was handsome, sensual, elegant, arresting, and delicate, and yet at the same time proud.

"Starting today," Cole said. "You two will be working together. And now, let's get back to work. We've got a lot of ground to cover."

The crowd dispersed as they patted Ross on the back.

# CHAPTER 3

CAROL BOLTON WAS A big Caucasian thirty-one-year-old girl who lived alone in a modest two-bedroom house on 137th Street and Tenth Avenue in North Miami, a middle-income community. She was alone partly because all her life she believed she was unattractive and overweight. But despite her weight problem, she continued to eat more than ever before. At four feet six inches tall, she had green eyes, a long face, jet-black long hair, and a supple body. As she sat at the table in front of an assortment of breakfast foods, she laughed and thought of her best friends' advice. "You have to do something about your weight, Carol," said Isabelle Palmer.

And the voice of Rachel Tolar also echoed in her head. "You just *have* to."

A few minutes later, Carol started to get ready for work, but she heard a familiar horn being honked. She ran to the window and looked out. Isabelle Palmer sat in her Camry yelling to Carol, "Hurry up, Carol! I'm running late."

"Be out in a second."

To her annoyance, Isabelle honked again.

When Carol finally made it inside the car, Isabelle was on the brink of exploding. "Jesus, Carol. Would you take a look at the clock?"

Isabelle was an exotic beauty with a sweet voice, full lips, long blonde hair, blue eyes, and a great body.

Carol said, "I know, girlfriend. Let's go."

Isabelle pulled the Camry away from the curb and went roaring down the street at breakneck speed. Tires spun and smoked. "This is every morning. And seatbelt, please."

Carol glared at Isabelle, bracing herself against the dashboard as they rounded a street corner. "What's happened? Didn't you get laid last night?" Carol asked as she pulverized a handful of nuts between her teeth.

"My social life is not your concern. I'm going to be late again. And Sal's going to let me go this time—for good."

Carol was looking in the mirror, applying more makeup. "He's not going to let you go," she droned on, heaping praise upon praise. "You're the best."


Seventeen-year-old Kim Leblanc groggily got up from a nap and snatched her cell phone from her bag. She was surprised she had actually heard the damned phone. For all she knew, she could sleep through Armageddon. "Hello?"

"Hello?"

Kim said, "Uh … who is this?"

"My name is Rick. Are you Kim?"

"Well, I'm Kim, but I have no idea who you are."

"I'm Rick Solomon, Gus's brother. And I'm calling about this parcel he left for me."

The other uptight prick, Kim thought bitterly. "Okay, but how do I know for sure you're Gus's brother?"

"Because he's got no other brother but me," snapped Rick.

Kim stretched and yawned. "All right, Rick," said Kim as petulance crept into her voice. "What exactly is in the parcel?"

"That's none of your business, Kim," said Rick.

"And what if I tell you he didn't give me squat for you, Rick?"

There was a pause on the other end of the line. Kim tried to hear a response. "Rick?"

And then he answered, "First I find you. Then I kill you. So, if I were you, I'd simply cooperate before I lose my temper."

Kim could not stand the audacity of the man. She tensed, but she didn't panic. "Really? Well, let me tell you something, Rick, or whatever your real name is," she said, sarcasm plumping out each word, "If you start giving me shit, you'll never get that parcel. In fact, I can hardly remember where the fuck it is."

Rick laughed. "Listen up, Kim," he said without emotion. "You want to keep that parcel, that's fine. But I know where you live. So, if you decide to play games with me, so help me God, you will be a dead girl within twenty-four hours. It's your choice. Look—"

"No, you look, prick. Who the hell are you threatening me like that?"

"Where is my parcel?"

"You want to get your parcel, you be nice, and you give me time to look for it. That's what you do."

Instead of saying yes or no, Rick shot back, "There was a time I used to be nice. I'm not nice anymore. So all I want you to do," instructed Rick, "is to place the parcel into a mailbox. The address is 59 West Thirteenth Street, Hialeah. I want it there by noon." Rick paused. "Hey, Kim, are you pretty?"

Kim blushed. "Just presentable."

"Very good. Well, if the parcel isn't there—59 West Thirteenth Street, Hialeah," he threatened again, "you won't be presentable anymore."

"Wait a minute," objected Kim, making useless gestures with her hand. And the line went dead.

Kim Leblanc had long, blonde hair, and blue-hazel eyes. Her smile was the whitest. The provocative way she swung her hips was enough to turn a gay man straight. She was five feet six inches tall. She weighed 125 pounds, and she had a slender body and a face that could make Marilyn Monroe look like rag. She had a nice ass and a gorgeous pair of legs connected to her twenty-eight-inch waist. But somehow she and her best friend, Sam, Gus's girlfriend, who was born fabulously wealthy, and at seventeen already thought of school as a boring interruption to her sex life, had begun seeing men and running the night clubs.

Kim rubbed the back of her neck and remembered the exact circumstances.

It all started on Kim's seventeen birthday, when Gus rolled a joint and offered it to her. At first, Kim politely declined. "I don't wanna do this, Gus," she said innocently. "They say it's very addictive."

"Come on, try it," encouraged Sam. "You'll like it. Trust me."

Gus nodded. "Yeah. Just don't inhale." He laughed as Sam took the joint and drew the smoke deep in her lungs. She handed it back to Kim.

Kim grimaced. "I don't think I should do this, Sam."

"It's good, gorgeous," suggested Gus lazily, now sampling cocaine on a glass table nearby. "Almost better than sex."

Sam fixed Kim with her glittering stoned eyes. "Hell, it's your birthday for crying out loud." She was blowing smoke rings in Kim's face. "Here," she said, handing her a joint. "It'll be okay."

Kim grabbed the joint and puffed on it but immediately started coughing and headed to the bathroom. When she returned, she found Gus and Sam doing coke. She looked at Gus in disbelief. "Isn't there anything you don't do?"

"I haven't done you." A lecherous smile crossed his face as Sam gave him a jealous stare. Gus then pointed his hand to the table.

"You want to try?"

He didn't have to ask her twice. And so it all began. What had started out as a routine soon changed into a habit. An unbreakable one. Later that night, they were driving back from a movie in Gus's car. It was not an option

18

that Kim preferred. She hated feeling trapped with no escape route. But Gus had something on mind and wouldn't take no for an answer. Sam said, "I thought the movie was good."

Gus deliberately picked a fight. "That movie sucked big green ones."

Sam said, "I guess it wasn't that good."

"Yes, I could have bought you a pizza with more drama."

Sam screamed. "I said it sucked."

The volume increased. "Yeah! And the next time we pick a movie, and you can read the comics."

"Fuck you," snarled Sam. Now they were on the verge of fighting. "You wanted the tits and ass on the screen."

"Shut the fuck up."

Sam dished it right back. "You shut the fuck up. Take me home. Now!"

"I'll kick your fuckin' ass."

"Take me home right now, or I'll walk home." They continued arguing until they arrived at Sam's house. She looked at Kim and then at Gus. "You asshole," she said, leaving Kim in the car with Gus.

As they drove away, Kim said, "I liked the movie, too."

Gus said, "I did, too."

"Then why did you do that to Sam?"

Gus was coming on to her strong as usual. "I'm falling in love with you, Kim," he announced dramatically. "And I can't help it."

Kim knew this was coming. "Gus," she said with great exaggeration and clutching her heart. "Sam is my best friend."

"I understand," he said, reasoning with her, "but you're so beautiful and understanding. Well, irresistible. And we're so much in sync."

"Yeah! And I'd look good sitting on your dick, right?"

"That too," he smiled, reaching out to delicately finger her pendant as if he had never seen it before. "This was my mother's," Kim murmured with a touch of wistfulness at never having really known her mother.

"Really?"

"Yeah."

Now Gus put the arm around her. The car swerved across the street. "How about a drink at my place? You know I also have a lot of coke and weed."

There was emptiness in her head.

"Aren't you afraid of getting caught?"

Gus pulled her closer to his seat as the car screeched to a halt at a flashing red light. "They will never take me alive."

Once she landed in his apartment, he dragged her to his king-size water bed and mounted her like a stallion. When they finished, Kim got dressed. Gus took hold of her shoulders, kissed her lips, and said, "I need a favor."

Kim stared at him, a puzzled look on her face. "Sure. You want a baby, too?"

Gus nodded. He let go of her shoulders, crossed the living room, and entered the kitchen. Right above the refrigerator, he unscrewed a panel from the ceiling and extracted a parcel from a paper bag. "And give my brother, Rick, this parcel."

"Why me and not Sam?"

"'Cause I trust *you* and not Sam. And I want you to hand deliver it. Can I count on you?"

Kim swore to secrecy. "How will I know him?"

Gus said, "He's the nice one in the family."

Two days later, Gus was killed. Sam and Kim were devastated. And now, she sat in her bed with a blank expression holding the parcel in her arms. Baffled, Kim surveyed the contents of the parcel: two rolls of one-hundred-dollar bills and a Gold MasterCard. She wrote down the credit card number. There was also a Hallmark envelope, a driver's license, and another large envelope containing about three pounds of heroin.

Kim kept the rolls of one-hundred-dollar bills and the heroin. "Kim don't work for free," she said excitedly. Then she sprang from the bed, breezed into the bathroom, splashed cold water on her face, peered in the mirror, and dressed quickly. In a minute, she would be out of the house and on her way to make the drop. But as she opened the front door, Ross was pulling into the driveway. A seriously handsome, clean-shaven stud was in the passenger seat.

An hour before, Ross gave Carl the grand tour of Miami. "I love my neighborhood."

Carl said, "Because it's quiet?"

"Because it's safe! We all know each other, and it's kind of like a big family."

"So what brought you to the city of doom?" Ross joked as they drove through the residential streets of Miami Shores, heading to Ross's house.

"I thought I was married to the love of my life."

Ross frowned. "If you don't mind, son," he said with sympathy, "what happened?"

"Caught her in bed with *her* girlfriend. And when I confronted her, she became a violent bitch."

"I'm sorry to hear that."

Carl shifted uneasily in the passenger's seat. "I was so hurt," he said, fighting back emotion. "I almost beat her to a pulp, but I'm not that type of guy."

Ross understood Carl had about him the air of a man who had known great loss and was capable of profound compassion.

He said, "I guess it would take a lot to change someone from being nice to cruel, wouldn't it?"

Carl nodded.

They drove in silence through beautiful single-family homes on tree-lined streets located on lush landscaping. Children played while parents indulged in friendly conversations. Located in Miami-Dade County, Miami Shores was a charming village that had a suburban feel, despite its proximity to downtown Miami. Carl decided to move there not only because he was guaranteed a job by his uncle, Captain Cole, but also he enjoyed the snow-white beaches, brilliant sunlit skies, sparkling blue waters, swaying palm trees, and the beautiful year-round weather. And there was never a shortage of fun things to do in Miami.

Vangelis was playing dreamily in the background. The addiction to their sound over the years had grown from a single to a whole collection. Ahead, at the intersection of Ninety-fifth Street and Biscayne Boulevard, a stoplight turned red, and Ross was unable to spare the inconvenience of braking. Strips of white clouds drifted lazily across the sky. The sun gazed down like an angry eye, while the temperature continued to rise into the nineties.

"Is that your wife on that boat?" Carl said, breaking the silence.

Ross was in deep thought. He had only heard the last word of the question. "Excuse me?"

"That woman in the key chain," repeated Carl. "Is she your wife?"

Ross was annoyed. He hated it when people inquired about September and made him feel obliged to say that she was dead. Sometimes he couldn't stand the sympathy in his friends' voices, for it was too much like leniency. "Yes."

"Beautiful woman."

"Thank you."

"What does she do?"

Ross bit his lower lip, avoiding eye contact. "She's dead."

"I'm sorry for your loss."

"We had seven wonderful months of marriage, and she passed on seven years ago."

"You have any kids?"

"Not with her, but I have a seventeen-year-old daughter."

"I see."

"She's beautiful and tells me everything," Ross said as he drove the car up to the head of his driveway. Red roses loomed at both sides of the entrance of the house.

Carl saw a beautiful young girl exiting the house. Ross said, "Speak of the same."

# CHAPTER 4

EXCEPT FOR A 1986 *Playboy* calendar in one corner, Rick's apartment was bare. But he didn't care because he didn't long for luxury. What mattered the most to him for now was privacy. After his conversation with Kim, he sat in bed going through his carryall bag, his only possession, and extracted a small notebook that looked the worse for the wear. He opened it to reveal pages of writing that consisted of just three letters: C.I.R. Then Rick removed a knife from a kitchen drawer, stepped upon a stool, and started carving letters into the ceiling. As he carved the *C*, he said, "Carol. I hope you like your new home." As he carved the *I*, he said, "And sometimes it doesn't pay to be a follower, Isabelle." And finally, as he carved the *R*, he said, "And rest assured, Rachel. You will be last." He stepped down to admire his handiwork. A cold smile crossed his lips. "And wherever you are, bimbos, I will find you."

Top Value Supermarket on Collins Avenue in Miami Beach was jam-packed. There must have been one hundred seniors inside, an equal mixture of Jews and whites, whose average age was at least seventy. Rachel Tolar slotted the Lexus into a parking space and made her way inside. There were long lines at each checkout. Lean and lithe, she approached a gentleman at the front desk, who was wearing a cheap red tie over a faded blue shirt. "Excuse me, sir. Is Carol around?"

"And what's your na—" He looked up, his eyes level at her breasts, which were disturbingly visible through her shirt. "Uh, name, ma'am?"

"Just Rachel will do."

Rachel watched him stare at her as he walked to the office. A moment later, Carol emerged from the office. "How did it go?" she asked, referring to the psychic reading.

"Apart from the cruise ship thing, I feel wonderful," she said, dropping her voice. "Invigorated."

"How could she see something like that," Carol asked. "Psychic powers, maybe?"

Rachel shrugged. "I guess. Anyway," she said, moving back to the original topic of conversation, "she's really good."

"That's great. Was she that accurate?" Carol said, eyes searching.

"Well, she told me to always be careful. And some memories flooded back. But the good news is," she confided, eyes gleaming with excitement, "Derek is going to marry me. And guess where?"

"Tell me."

"On a cruise ship."

"Oh my God!"

Rachel changed the subject. "Don't worry about it. What time are you off today?"

"Two. Three. Vacation time, remember?"

"Well, don't eat too much!"

"Hey, have your orgasms. I'll have mine."

They both laughed and threw their arms around each other.

Spinning on her heels, Rachel swept out of the supermarket and drove to Sal's Deli on Seventy-ninth Street and Collins to see Isabelle Palmer. But as she reached the intersection on Seventy-first and Collins, her heart jumped into her throat as she nearly killed an elderly woman who was attempting to cross the street. A wave of panic left her shaking all over. She sat at the side of the road and cried.

Sal Gamini greeted Rachel with a megawatt smile and a kiss on her cheek. "Rachel, how are you today?"

"I'm doing fine, Sal. You?"

"I'm fine. You look great," he said, a definite come-on in his voice. In his midfifties, he seemed to have invested a lot of time and money in the maintenance of a youthful appearance.

"Thank you."

He eyed her up and down with interest. "Can I get you a drink?"

"No, thanks. I came to see Bella real quick."

"She's not here."

"Why?"

Sal placed a flirtatious hand over her shoulder. "Didn't you hear?"

"Hear what?"

"Her brother-in-law from Jacksonville was shot. They called her here."

Another wave of panic struck Rachel. She felt suddenly weak and nerveless. "When did that happen?"

Sal looked at his watch and gazed around. The place was packed. Patrons stood patiently in line to get a table. "Uh, about an hour ago. As much as I need her, I had to let her go. Family comes first, right?"

The combination of the psychic reading, the near-miss accident, and Sal's bad news generated in Rachel an eerie sense of expectancy.

"Sure you don't want anything?" Sal asked.

Rachel shook her head. "No, thanks, Sal. I'm going to go see her before she leaves."

Carrying a bag, Kim walked up to her dad and Carl. She greeted her dad first. "Hi, Dad."

"Hey, kiddo," said Ross proudly. "How are you?"

Kim loathed it when her dad called her kiddo, especially when she was about to meet such a handsome stud.

She displayed her killer smile. "Fine."

"Kim," he said, "this is Detective Carl Levy. Carl, this is my daughter, Kim."

"Pleased to meet you, Detective Levy."

They shook hands formally. Kim's skin was immediately tingling, every nerve alert. Holy mackerel! Carl was more attractive up close. She curbed a wild impulse to reach out and kiss him fully on the lips. Instead, she held herself, body and soul, in a vise of iron, trying not to be waylaid too much by his charm, which wasn't easy.

"Please call me Carl."

And for a split second, they held each other's gaze. Kim's heart swelled with an undefined fullness. All at once, her sexual senses were assailed on every level. Ross asked her a question that jolted her back to reality: "How come you're not in school?"

Kim's eyes pulled away from Carl's. "I had a field trip. I'm on my way back, Dad."

"All right," Ross said. "Just be home early. Carl is having dinner with us."

"Yes, Dad. I'll be here on time."

"You should be because I'm taking you on a cruise this weekend."

Kim's face turned red with excitement. Her eyes lit up like a child's at Christmas. "Really?"

"This Sunday. Here," he said, fishing out his wallet and handing her three crisp one-hundred-dollar bills, "buy what you think you'll need."

"Thanks, Dad!"

She disposed a jammy kiss on Ross's cheek and turned to Carl. "Nice meeting you." Then she jumped in her car and pulled out onto the street.

Thirty minutes later, Kim arrived in Hialeah. With the parcel in hand, she stepped out of the car, looked around, spotted an old and rusty mailbox on a wooden post in front of an abandoned duplex, raced across the sidewalk, and placed the parcel inside. Then she closed the mailbox and got back in her car. As she drove away, she looked in the rearview mirror to see if anyone saw her. But there was no one until she made a turn to an open street. With several thousand dollars in Kim's possession, the prospect of shopping was quite appealing. From her car, she punched Sam's number. The phone was picked up on the fourth ring. "Hello."

"Meet me in Aventura in twenty minutes."

Sam said, "What for?"

"Two things: I need to go to Sprint to have my number changed. And you need to help me pick out some clothes for a cruise."

"Wow! Number changed? A cruise?"

"I'll explain. Just be there," Kim said, fingering the several thousand dollars lying on the seat beside her.

In less than an hour, Kim and Sam walked out of a Sprint service shop. Kim played with her phone. Each carried a bag of clothes. "I really don't know why you changed your number, girl."

Kim lied. "I told you. The prick said he's going to slit my throat."

"Did you tell your dad?"

"I can handle my own men. And speaking of men," she continued chattily, "my dad's partner is my next fuck."

Sam glared at Kim. "What. You're going to fuck your dad's partner? Girl, you've got issues."

# CHAPTER 5

RICK THREW THE CONTENTS of the parcel on the bed. Then he opened a Hallmark envelope and removed a letter and a newspaper clipping. As he silently read the letter from his brother, his face lit up. He read the last part of the letter aloud: "Need anything else at all, go see Sean at the Kaleidoscope nightclub in South Beach. He's a good friend of mine. Your brother, Gus."

Rick looked at the clipping and then at the letter. "The broad's too stupid to know what she didn't steal."

Stunned, Rick picked up the phone and called Kim. He listened for Kim's voice but ended up with a computer-generated response instead: "The number you dialed is no longer in service."

While Kim was having her way with Rick's money, Rick Solomon was on slow burn, furious at the situation. Another spiteful woman had done him wrong. His stomach churned. Something dark was boiling inside him. He wished he could find the girl right then and beat her like a circus monkey. But he decided not to get carried away too much. He was certain he'd find and punish her. As Kim made the drop in the mailbox, which was located right across the street from his room, he had watched her every move and had even written down her license plate number. Her eyes had darted in all directions, as if thieves were lurking behind her. Had Rick known that she was a thief, he could have come out and abducted her. Lesson learned. He smiled with a hint of anger and sadism. "You can change your number, but you can't change you."

Rick worked on his appearance and even cut his hair to his scalp. Shortly after that, he went out and rented a minivan. At Kmart, he loaded bags of clothes, suitcases, and necessities into the back of the minivan. He was a man who planned ahead. He took out some Ray-Ban sunglasses and tried them out, first putting them on and then taking them off. He liked what he saw.

Moving away from Kmart, Rick steered the minivan onto 441, heading south. He stopped in a pawnshop, worked out a deal with the owner, and bought a .32-caliber pistol with a sound suppressor, which was illegal, but the owner didn't care. He also bought ammo and a knife. "You two are ready to meet my friends," Rick said softly to himself, as though the gun and knife could hear him.

Satisfied, he drove south and entered the eighth-of-a-mile lane leading him onto Interstate 95, exited on Seventy-ninth Street, and headed east to North Bay Village via John Fitzgerald Kennedy Causeway. Driving thirty-five miles per hour, he made it to Top Value Supermarket on Collins Avenue in twenty minutes. The temperature was hitting ninety-one degrees in Miami Beach. Even with a breeze coming off the ocean, the humidity was so oppressive that just standing in one place was almost like swimming through thick, dense air. Rick thought he was going to have a freaking stroke. Inside the supermarket was a madhouse. People were buying lottery tickets for the next day's drawing. Some were cashing checks. Others were paying for groceries. He looked at the many cashiers behind the registers. "Where are you, Carol? You fat little fart."

Rick's mind jumped to images of Carol wearing her uniform as she took the witness stand. He wondered if she was still uncaring, intense, and audacious, and how would time have changed her. Rick pushed a cart farther into the market to see if he might spot her somewhere else. Deep in thought, he surveyed the frenzy of activities that took place at the front desk. There was no sign of Carol. Rick paid for the groceries and made for the exit. As he wheeled the cart with several bags out of the market, a bag boy appeared. "I'll take that," the boy said.

"I can do it," Rick said.

The boy, who just wanted to earn a tip, said, "Carryout service is our policy, sir."

Rick considered a possibility and gave him the go ahead. "Hey, my car's over there," he said, holding out a five dollar bill, impressing with his own generosity. "And this is yours if you can answer a question for me."

The boy smiled.

"I'm looking for a heavyset woman named Carol Bolton. Do you know her?"

The boy nodded. "Carol is my boss. She's going on vacation tomorrow. And between me and you, I hope she's never coming back because she's truly a pain in my ass."

Rick patted the boy on his shoulder and said, "Young man, your wish is my command."

Isabelle Palmer was at home packing clothes when the doorbell rang. She walked to the door and found Rachel standing there, looking worried. Rachel hurried in and hugged Isabelle. "I came when I heard."

"That's what friends are for."

Rachel said, "Does Carol know?"

More than three years ago, these three girls made a covenant to remain together always and to share all.

"No. I found out at work." Bella said, taking her arm and gently shoved her onto the couch.

"How?"

"Three men tried to rob Jim at the bank. They traded shots. He's in critical condition. Care for a drink?"

"I'm not really thirsty, but—" She changed her mind as she looked at Bella's drink. "Add some coke to what you're drinking."

Isabelle walked over to the kitchen, reached into a cabinet, and extracted a bottle of vodka. She fixed Rachel a drink.

"When are you going?" Rachel asked.

"I'm going up tomorrow."

Isabelle returned with the drink and handed it to Rachel.

"I'm taking a couple of weeks off."

"A couple of weeks without pay?"

Bella lit up a cigarette, tapped impatient buff nails on the table as if she was in deep thought. Her sweet voice droned on, "My sister needs me. Can't put a price on love."

Rachel rubbed her hand for a little while and then whipped out her checkbook. "Here," she said, handing Isabella a check.

"I can't afford a loan, either."

Rachel grabbed her purse and rose from the couch. "It's not a loan. It's part of your share."

"And I didn't want a share."

Rachel hugged her and said, "But you helped make it happen."

Isabelle walked Rachel to the front door. "I still didn't want a share."

Rachel ignored the comment. She climbed inside her car, a green Lexus coupe of the latest style, buckled her seatbelt, and said, "This, too, shall pass."

As Rachel drove away, Isabelle felt the past once again. It never went away. Never.


Rachel waited patiently at the elevators of her high-security condominium when suddenly a voice was heard. "You always hang out in lobbies."

She turned in panic and then breathed a sigh of relief when she saw that it was Derek. She said, "Only to meet strange men."

They kissed as they entered the elevator. She looked at Derek seductively.

"You hungry?"

"Hungry? I could eat the ass out of a dead rhinoceros."

The elevator door closed.

"What's wrong with my ass?"

Smiling, Derek gave Rachel a prefatory pinch on the ass. "That's for dessert."

The elevator jerked and stopped on the tenth floor. The door whooshed open. "Will it be the same tomorrow?" she teased, recalling their earlier conversation after her psychic reading. They stepped out of the elevator and made their way to her suite. Derek changed the subject as they went inside. "Speaking of tomorrow. I'm hungry today."

Rachel placed her bag on the kitchen counter, picked up the phone, and punched in a number. "Let me make a quick two calls, and then I promise you a delicious dessert."

Derek sat on the couch. "Be careful what you ask for."

Rachel winked at him. "Beverly. Glad I caught you. I want to bring a guest to my tennis lesson tomorrow. Carol Bolton. But she thinks a vacation is the time to spend sampling the eight food groups daily. Great! I'll call her right now."

As Derek played with the television's remote, Rachel punched in Carol's number. All the while she was unbuttoning her blouse, teasing Derek. Derek caught a glimpse and licked his lips. She smiled seductively at Derek. "Let me call Carol, and then the whipped cream will begin."

Carol's phone rang and rang. No answer. Rachel hung up the phone. "I guess she's not home."

Derek walked up behind Rachel, who was standing with no blouse on, just her bra. "Her loss, not mine," Derek said.

Meanwhile, Carol Bolton talked to her cat, Natasha, as she removed her uniform. "Two weeks off with soap operas and food," she said, holding up a can of gourmet tuna. "And I got you some special kitty food, too."

Suddenly, there was a knock at the door. "Someday, I'll get my shower. Who's there?" Then a male voice rang out: "It's about your car, ma'am. Is it still for sale or not?"

She tensed as she looked through the fish-eye peephole. As far as she could see, it was a decent-looking gentleman. "Just a sec."

She put on a robe, removed the security chain, and opened the door. "Can you come ba—"

She never finished her statement, as she was struck in the face and fell backward onto the floor.

# CHAPTER 6

To RICK, TRACKING DOWN Carol Bolton was as easy as a walk in the park. From his minivan he watched Carol come back from lunch and then leave the supermarket with a middle-aged woman. Rick followed them all the way back to North Miami, keeping an appropriate distance behind them until they pulled into the driveway of a brown single-story house. Carol got out of the car, spoke to the woman for a couple of minutes, and sent her away. Rick slowly cruised past and noticed a wrecked Pontiac in the lawn with a For Sale sign plastered on the window. Because it was still daylight, Rick was buoyed by the possibility of paying a visit to Carol later at night. But as he drove through the neighborhood, there was hardly anyone around. The area was quiet and the timing was just perfect.

Rick knelt down and talked to an unconscious Carol. "Now I'm going to teach you something about the value of life and respect for the innocent. Nice and slow."

The telephone rang in the background.

Rick said, "No one's home."

A terrified Carol tried to move. But both her wrists were manacled to the headboard of the bed. Her head felt like it had been struck by a sledgehammer. She felt naked, but she wasn't sure. But when did that happen? She didn't know. It all happened so fast. So quick. Maybe this was a dream. Wincing, she forced her eyes to slowly open, only to see the shadow of a man wearing sunglasses sitting across from her. Jesus! And it all came to her. She'd been abducted. She blinked and gasped in shock. "Oh no!"

"Oh yes!" said the decent-looking gentleman. "And long time no see, uh!"

"Who are ... you?" Carol's heart was racing. Her throat was choked with fear, making it hard for her to speak. "And what ... do you want from me?"

The man stared at her, eyes unreadable behind dark Ray-Ban sunglasses.

"Just take whatever you want," stuttered a frantic Carol. "And leave me alone."

"Do I look like a thief to you?"

Carol repeated. "Who are you, then?"

"You don't remember? I'm hurt."

"So what do you want from me?"

"Actually respect ... but the truth, only the truth will do for now. So you tell me the truth, you'll live. And if you don't, I'm going to have to kill you ... slowly."

"What truth?"

The man ignored the question. He extracted a pack of chewing gum from his pocket. "You care for one?"

Carol shook her head. And the man said, "I didn't think so. But anyway, the bag boy said you are an overzealous asshole, and I don't care. I'm here to ask you if you were given a choice between life and death, which one would you prefer? And be honest."

Carol's head swam in a fog of terror. She said, "I ... I ... want life. I want to live. I'll tell you whatever ... you need to know. P-please, mister. Don't kill me."

The decent-looking man got up and walked over to Carol. "It's good to know you want to live, but if you lie to me ..." His voice was scornful and getting louder. "What I'm going to do is very simple. See this knife?" He waved the blade across her face. It was sharp as an ice pick. "If you don't tell me everything I need to know, I'm going to cut out your tongue and make you swallow it." He paused, removing the blade from her face, and strolled back to his chair.

A new wave of fear swept over Carol. "No!"

"Not the answer I want to hear. Do you understand, Carol? Do we have an agreement here?"

She wanted to say, "Asshole." But she didn't dare. Instead, she mouthed a cold and silent, *Okay*.

"Okay what? Dialogue? Or your tongue? It's your decision."

"Dialogue. T-that's what I meant."

"Good," he said, smiling. "I'd like to start it off with a short story. Is that okay with you?"

Carol nodded.

"All right! My grandmother used to tell me that if you lie to help someone out, the mighty God will forgive you. But," he said piously, raising his finger up in the air, "if you lie to harm someone, you should be punished. I mean harshly."

A wily alertness crept into Carol's eyes as she recognized the face of the man before her. "Rick …" Terror now gripped Carol. "Oh, God."

"Don't ask for His help. I'm God today. And my sermon is going to be on revenge. So, now you're going to tell me. Why me?"

Carol grabbed for words. Her face was a mask of indescribable fear.

"It was all a mistake," said a confused, thunderstruck Carol.

Rick convulsed with laughter. "Come on now, Carol, just between us two here, let's be honest for once. You knew darned well I didn't do it. Didn't you?"

Carol shook her head in acknowledgement.

Rick was enjoying every minute of his encounter. "Then why me?"

Carol was speechless. Rick's eyes grew fierce with anger as he waited for her answer. "Then why me?" he repeated. "Fates intertwined? Coincidence? Or being in the wrong place at the wrong time? Just amazing." He was making gestures with his shoulders and hands as he spoke. "But you know why it happened?" said Rick, staring at her with obvious hatred. "Because I was being nice. I was a damned Good Samaritan and ran to her assistance. That's why. And what did I get back in return? Three fucking years behind bars. Could you imagine that? Being in prison for something you didn't do?"

He paused. "So, all I need to know is why did she do it?"

An eerie silence cloaked the entire bedroom. There was a cold feeling in Carol's gut, as though mercury had pooled there. Watching Rick now with a flinty, hard look that had such a dangerous edge to it made her whole body numb. She closed her eyes, praying, willing time to turn back, willing things to change, wishing that their lives had turned out differently three years ago. If only they hadn't been on that ship at the very same time.

Rick screamed, "Answer me!"

Carol blinked furiously, clearing tear-blurred vision. Anger sizzled in every vein.

"It was Rachel's lawyer that made us do it. I swear."

"Ah, her lawyer." Rick stared into her exhausted eyes. "Were you all born with something called a conscience maybe?"

"I'm sorry, Rick," muttered Carol. "Please forgive me."

Rick nodded understandingly. "Okay, here's the deal: you tell me where to find Rachel, and I let you live."

Carol hesitated, and then she lied, "Honestly, I-I don't know where she is."

"You don't know," echoed Rick. "You folks aren't friends anymore?"

Carol said, "No."

"Why not?"

"After the trial, she changed and moved to West Palm. She's rich now. She don't need me."

"She used you, too," Rick said with sarcasm. "And you don't think she deserves to be punished?"

"That's up to you, Rick. But I think, Mike, her lawyer, he should be punished. I-I mean, he should be dead. Not us. I didn't even know you. But he put pressure on us, said that if Isabelle and I cared about our friend, we must testify against you."

Rick nodded. "Oh, I see. And where is Isabelle?"

"She moved, too," said Carol, trying with all her might to show no weakness in her voice.

"Where to?" growled Rick.

"Orlando."

"She moved, too? All your friends are moving, and you're still here? You know something, Carol?" Rick said without emotion. "You've proven to be a true friend. Don't you think it's about time to let them know that?"

Carol fell silent as Rick made his way toward the kitchen, only to return with her address book. Carol trembled. Her heart pounded, making the veins in her neck and wrist pulse.

"I see the area code for Rachel and Isabelle is for Miami. Is that also an error?"

She lied again. "It's an old book."

Rick shut the address book and dropped it on the floor. "Too many lies, Carol."

Carol stared at him with varying degrees of hostility and disbelief as Rick stood up and stripped off his shirt and shrugged his pants off, letting them fall to the floor. Moving in her direction, Rick removed his briefs, revealing his stiff prick. Hate, shame, regret all boiled up inside her. She prayed for the rape to be over quickly.

Rick said, "How about one for the team, eh?"

"You sick bastard," Carol said, surprised to find a drop of hostility remaining in her vast pool of resignation and sorrow. "You'll never get away with this. Next time they'll hang you."

Rick laughed. It was a malevolent laugh, one that frightened Carol even more than before. "I won't be long. Three hours or less maybe."

"Fuck you, asshole." That was Carol's last act of defiance.

Rick ignored her outbursts and climbed onto the bed. Carol knew that she was about to experience her worst nightmare.

Carl Levy was fast asleep when the phone rang. Either his ex-wife died and went straight to hell with a one-way ticket, or a rape had occurred and Ross was in hot pursuit. Who else would call at such hour? "Hello?"

"Carl? It's Kim."

"Beg your pardon?" he mumbled sleepily.

"It's Kim, Ross's daughter. You just had dinner with us, remember?"

"Oh, Kim," he said, sitting up and reaching for a light. The sudden brightness of the fluorescent made him squint. "Is everything all right?"

He glanced at his watch: 1:31 AM.

"Yeah, everything is fine."

"So, uh, what's up?"

"Uh, I just need someone to talk to."

"At this time in the morning?"

"No. I want you to come to the house tomorrow morning."

Feeling awkward and stupid for his reaction, Carl said, "I don't understand."

Kim said, "I know, but you're the only person I can trust." And as if it was an afterthought, she added, "It's very important."

Carl hesitated. "But—"

"Don't worry about Dad," she reassured. "He doesn't have a clue about what I do. In fact, he'll be playing golf tomorrow. So can I count on you or not?"

Just his luck. "Yeah, yeah, sure," he said reluctantly.

"So, I'll see you tomorrow morning at ten, right?"

"Sure."

Carl looked at the receiver and pondered his dilemma. His head was spinning slowly as he closed his eyes and drifted back to sleep.

# CHAPTER 7

RACHEL TOLAR OPENED HER eyes and stared at the dimly lit ceiling of her luxurious apartment. She turned her head to the right. The numerals of the alarm clock put the time at 7:33 AM. She tried to move. "Oh, shit," she whispered softly, trying to deny the sharp jab of pain that always came in the morning after she and Derek had a long and rough night of passion. The framed photographs on her nightstand left no room for anything but a lamp and the alarm clock. She gazed at the pictures for a moment. Some of them brought back good memories, and some didn't. Derek was in bed next to her, the sheets rumpled around his athletic body. He was snoring like a baby cat. Rachel stared at her future husband's face in the soft glow of the bedside lamp and felt a warm flood of delight.

She pushed the sheet away and eased slowly from the bed. Careful not to make any noise, she walked into the bathroom, making a quarter-turn to go through the doorway and closing the door softly behind her. A quick leak in slow motion followed by a quick shower. Then she toweled herself dry, stared at her reflection, picked up a comb, and swiped gently at her blonde hair before she applied a little makeup.

When she finished in the bathroom, she went to the closet for a change of white Nike sweats and tennis shoes. Then she made her way into the kitchen, grabbed the phone, and called Carol. As the phone rang, she reached for the refrigerator with one hand and extracted a gallon of skim milk. She poured herself half a glass and downed it with three long gulps. After ten rings with no answer, Rachel hung up the phone and put the glass into the kitchen sink. The kitchen counter needed a bit of cleaning, but she could not be bothered now to stoop to the chore. Instead, she picked up her handbag and car keys, and took off.

Twenty minutes later, Rachel was in North Miami. That morning was fantastic, with a blue sky, light wind, blazing sunshine, and the temperature hovering in the low eighties. A true tropical climate. It was exactly 9:03 AM as she walked up to Carol's front door. Confidently, she knocked on the door.

Nobody responded.

She knocked again.

Nothing.

She peered through the front window. "Carol, are you in there?"

The place seemed deserted, and Carol didn't answer. A shiver shot down Rachel's spine. She found the door unlocked and pushed it open. The hinge made a screechy sound that sent a chill from her toes to her spine. But the door was held back by an obstruction. She nervously reached down to remove the obstacle as she entered and found herself screaming at the sight of the cat's brains spilling all over the carpet. Her stomach tightened up, and her skin turned cold. She looked out the door, thinking she should run, but she quickly decided against it. Rachel's legs grew weak as she stepped into the house and walked through the kitchen and down the hall. "Carol, are you in here?"

There wasn't a sound.

Nothing. Silence.

In the back of Rachel's mind, she knew that she should calm down. Losing it now was not going to help either Carol or herself. But with the sight of the dead cat and the silent house pressing in on her, she was temporarily incapable of rational behavior.

"Carol, please answer me."

No response.

Five seconds passed. Ten. Fifteen. Thirty.

A thin film of sweat formed on her brow. She was fighting back tears, shaking, and struggling to keep her mounting fear at bay as she entered the guest bathroom. It was dark. She fumbled for the light switch and clicked it on. Soft light illuminated the bathroom. The room was clean, but Rachel stared at the shower curtain. She hesitated, and then she drew the curtain back. Nothing. Drops of water made a soft *tink* as they fell from the shower faucet onto the metal topper of the tub.

Rachel's fear increased as she backed out of the bathroom, took two steps across the hall, and stood in front of the door of the master bedroom. A fly buzzed behind her ear, startled her. Panic-stricken, she turned around too fast and almost lost her balance. She was chilled, drenched in sweat, and little speckles were dancing on the insides of her eye. "Stay calm," she told herself. "Stay cool." *Carol probably got away the minute she realized an intruder was in the house. She's all right*, Rachel thought.

Rachel twisted the doorknob, but the sweat on her hand made it slick. She wiped her hand on her clothes and turned the knob again. She hesitated, trying to build up enough courage to open the bedroom door. Suddenly, the bolt snapped open with a hard *clink*. She winced as the spring latch scraped softly out of its notch, and she pushed the door open just a crack, prepared to slam it shut at the slightest sign of movement.

But she didn't open the bedroom door. Couldn't. Not yet. True terror lay in the anticipation of the unknown.

The suspense was getting unbearable. A coldness rose in the pit of her stomach. Her breath quick-frozen in her lungs, each beat of her heart was like the concrete-busting of a jackhammer. *Open the damned door, for fuck's sake!* she thought. She realized that she had been hesitating for a couple of minutes. *Carol is not dead in there. And there's nothing to be worried about.* She had to prove herself that nothing had happened to Carol. She had to prove herself that even though she had been a coward, a nervous wreck all her life, deep down she was strong and never ran away from trouble. So, she *must* go in.

Taking a deep breath, she opened the door wider—two inches, three inches, four inches—expecting to see nothing but Carol's neat and organized bedroom. But when she looked inside, she could not believe what she saw and did not know how to react to it, other than with disgust and horror. Carol's mutilated body was nailed to the bed's headboard like Jesus on the cross. Her mouth had been sliced open several times. It protruded grotesquely, with hideous blisters on the upper lip. Her nose was swollen, streaked with blood. White sticky suppuration that could be sperm was coagulated all over her face. The blood and knife wounds created a road map on her body. She appeared to have died slowly and to have been dead for several hours.

Gagging with revulsion, Rachel stumbled backward one step, bile rising in her stomach. She didn't dare to look at the corpse. She tried to puke but couldn't. Her throat instantly seemed to be clogged, as if she was being swept away by a frozen and turbulent river, suffocating in its bitter waters, fighting for breath but finding none. She plunged back into the hall to the living room, staggered, and nearly fell. Her legs muscles felt like they were on fire. Grief welled up in her, black and cold. The heavy beat of her heart was too much to bear. She felt like she'd been kicked in the stomach by a thousand horses.

Shuffling forward, she managed to reach the kitchen. The front door, her only escape, seemed like it was a mile away. Her legs felt like they weighed a million tons. Rachel gasped, unable to get enough breath, as if the air was thick or full with acrid smoke. Her throat was raw. Never had she felt so sick at heart. Her head was spinning, and her entire being became still. Unable to go on, she huddled against the wall. Her head shook so much, she felt like she might crumble into a million pieces. It took her a superhuman effort to crawl outside to get help. By the time a neighbor arrived, she was numb, exhausted, and in shock.

When Carl slotted the car into Ross's driveway, it was almost ten o'clock in the morning. Reaching the front door, he rang the bell. The door opened, and Carl stood in awe of Kim. She was wearing a see-through skirt and a cutoff blouse that barely made it across her boobs. Her blonde hair was all loose and wet. Kim ran into his arms and walked away just as fast. "Come on in and sit down." Her voice was rich and full.

Carl sat down and got straight to the point. "So, what is it you want to tell me about?"

Kim dropped onto the couch next to him. "Dad said you're single and looking."

Carl tried with all his might to remain self-control. "Why is that important to you?"

And she moved still closer, and her blouse fell open, revealing her breasts. "Because it could be good for us both," she said, revealing a dazzling row of beautiful teeth.

Carl laughed halfheartedly. As a detective, he saw uncertainty in this peculiar situation, the possibility that he was being bluffed or toyed with, and a certain dawning of a logical assumption: she had something else in mind besides sex. "How so?" he asked.

"'Cause ... I've—"

Kim stopped as if she were unsure of how to go on.

Carl waited. *Sometimes you can't help people. Sometimes it's better not even to try,* Carl thought.

"I've, well, you and I have a very strong connection." Her voice was soft and dreamy.

"Really?" he said, trying to avoid gazing into her open blouse.

Kim nodded, her eyes fastened on Carl.

"I don't think your dad, who's my new partner, would feel the same way."

Kim was silent. An emotional dip of her head set the blonde wet curls to dancing sideways. One hugged her neck and draped across an olive swell of breast.

"So aside from the seduction, what else brought me here?" Carl asked, anxious to diffuse the sexually charged situation.

His comment worked. The mood changed. Kim's smile dropped off her face the way that writing comes off a blackboard wiped with a wet sponge. She said, "Can I trust you?"

Carl watched her with keen anticipation. "Of course."

"I met this ... well, two weeks ago I had spent one night with a drug dealer named Gus, who gave me a parcel for his brother, Rick, to hold until Rick got out of prison. Two days later, Gus died. Rick called me yesterday and threatened me. He said if I don't have the parcel in some mailbox in Hialeah by noon, I won't be pretty anymore."

Carl had never heard of the place before. "Hia what?"

"Hialeah," repeated Kim slowly.

"Did you?" he asked. "Did you give him the parcel?"

Kim bit her lower lip. "I did, but I accidentally nicked some money and a bag of heroin from it. And I feel guilty and a bit scared in case he finds out, you know?"

Carl was shocked, too surprised to utter a word for a long moment. Kim started talking again before he could respond.

"I'm sorry to dump this on you like that, Carl. It's terrible of me, but—"

For a moment more Carl stared, and then got angry, which did his head no good whatsoever. "You know I'm a cop, right?"

"And if you say anything, then I'll clam up, but I want to get it fixed."

"Your dad know?"

She groaned. "Oh no. He'd go into cardiac arrest."

"So you want me to fuck my career up?"

Kim placed her hands on his. "No. I don't. But I need some advice."

Carl felt uneasy. The kind of feeling that he hated. "You should never have ripped off the bad guys. They will hurt you. So, if you don't give it to me, then give it back."

Her lips moved in languid protest. "No, no, I can't."

Carl laughed. "Why not?"

"Because I have the heroin, but I already spent a lot of the money."

Carl shook his head as his cell phone rang. "Give me a moment," he said to Kim. "Officer Levy speaking."

"Hey, Carl, we've got a vic up in North Miami. You and Ross just caught the case. He will meet you there after he heads home."

Carl tensed a bit. "Sure, Captain."

"Because Ross is going on vacation, you're in charge."

*Oh, great,* thought Carl. *Just great.* Then he looked at Ross's daughter.

"I'm in route, sir!"

He closed his cell and faced Kim.

"Do yourself a favor, Kim. Call Rick and apologize. Tell him you're sorry for what happened and that the heroin is still untouched and ready to be delivered."

Kim quickly moved close to Carl and kissed him on the cheek. It was just a quick peck. Nothing more, nothing less.

"Carl, will you think about me?"

Carl was on his feet. "How can I forget about you?"

Carol's bedroom smelled of blood, burnt powder, and an overwhelming stench of human waste. *The smell was always the same when some asshole slaughtered another human being,* Carl thought. Carl and Ross put on gloves as they walked around Carol's bed. Carl looked closely at Carol's Top Value Supermarket tag. A technician took pictures as officer Leon Perez guarded the door. Ross started to ask an officer already on the scene some questions.

"Any evidence of forced entry?"

"No, sir," the officer said. "Looks like she let the killer in."

The technician was a short, thin, and impish-looking redhead of about thirty. He moved closer to the body and took some more pictures.

"Any fingerprints, notes, marks?" Ross asked the technician.

Without looking back at Ross, the technician shot back, "Nothing."

Ross and Carl got the immediate impression that the technician was clearly unimpressed by both the scene and detectives who outranked him.

"Well? What you got?" Ross asked another technician, who had just walked in from another room holding out a plastic bag to Ross with a piece of paper from a small notebook. "Looks like the perp left us a love note."

Ross turned the bag so that he could read the note. Carl watched. "We have a patriot," Ross said.

"A patriot?" Carl asked, looking puzzled.

"The note says that he's bringing justice to America and the Pledge of Allegiance."

Carl paced around the bed. The body was about to be removed from the bed headboard for placement in a body bag. He looked about with an expert eye, tapped his lower lip thoughtfully with his finger. "What do you think, Ross?"

Ross said, "Whoever wrote this note had a lot of time. Each letter is blocked, so his handwriting can't be analyzed."

The lab technician said, "And the guy plans ahead. Left absolutely no trace except the note. And to complicate matters, he also left the front and back doors unlocked. The back one was left wide open."

Ross gave an optimistic smile. "He'll fuck up."

And to Ross's annoyance, officer Leon Perez added, "Don't we all?"

Ross glared at Leon. He was a scruffy type with red cheeks, long sideburns, and thick limbs, with the look of a man who could make your blood run cold. Carl felt an underlying tension between the two officers.

Choosing to ignore Leon's sarcasm, Ross said, "This was personal and nothing else."

"And this guy's a bastard with the heart of a canned ham," added the lab technician as he removed his gloves.

42

Carl took a handkerchief from his pocket and wiped sweat from his forehead. He looked at Ross and said, "I'm not sure."

Ross said, "Look around. Everything in the house is in order. Her purse is intact—money, credit cards, address book, makeup — the whole nine yards." Every eye turned upon him now. "This incident is strictly a message of hate. I can vouch for that. Now, he must have been watching her—"

"Or he used the element of surprise," finished the lab technician for Ross.

"Exactly," boasted Ross, looking at Carl. "And that's why I'm not going on vacation tomorrow. I want this case until it's solved."

Carl frowned. "I thought—"

Ross stepped forward, shouldering Carl aside. "There will be other cases, Carl, but I want this one."

"You mean you don't trust me?" Carl said in protest. "I've worked homicide before."

"I know," Ross said. "But now I need you to question Rachel Tolar again. Please."

Carl nodded sullenly as Carol's body was being removed from her restraints. He wondered whether or not Ross's willingness to take over the case when he was about to leave for vacation was personal. For about a minute, he stood there watching other lab men comb the place, unsure about what was going on with Ross.

Carl stepped out of the house. He found Rachel sitting in a porch chair and crying. By then a large crowd had gathered outside. Residents jostled one another beyond a police barrier of taut yellow crime-scene tape to have a better look. Newscasters from several TV stations were reporting on the event live. More cops poured into the area, flashing their emergency beacons and sealing off the entire block. It seemed that in the space of five minutes, the entire State of Florida had been notified.

"I'm very sorry about your friend," said Carl in a soft, encouraging voice, "but I need to ask you more questions."

Rachel shook her head as she wiped tears away from her eyes. "No. I have had enough for now. I've got to go home. I need some sleep."

"Look," said Carl, placing a friendly hand on her shoulder. "I know how you feel. But we need your help."

Slowly Rachel turned to Carl, her grainy, hot, and exhausted eyes told so much. She said, "Have you ever had a very close friend of yours brutally murdered?"

"No, ma'am."

"Then you can't possibly know how I feel."

"I apologize. I'll ask you questions later."

Carl handed her a card, helped her get up, and walked her to her Lexus. He opened the driver's side door for her, allowing her to ease back into the leather seat and shut the door.

"At least answer me just one question for now," Carl asked through the open driver's side window.

Rachel fastened her seatbelt. "If it can't wait."

"How did Carol get to work?"

Rachel started the engine, closed her eyes, and leaned back in her seat, revealing the curves of her supple body. Carl was captivated by her beauty, even though there were bags under her eyes you could pack clothes in.

"My friend Isabelle picked her up."

"Thank y—"

Rachel drove away.

"Thank you very much, Rachel. I appreciate all your cooperation. Because it will allow us to catch the perp before he kills again," Carl muttered, the sarcasm plain in his voice. He shook his head as Rachel hung a short U-turn, dodged the many police cars, and disappeared at the intersection. He was about to have a long and busy Saturday.


Ross burst into the office as Cole sat with his back to the door. "I'd like to cancel my vacation plans," Ross said. "I want this case."

Cole swiveled his chair around to confront Ross. "That's a negative, Ross."

"Why not?"

Cole removed his glasses. "Because you are now on vacation. When you get back from your cruise, Carl will turn it over to you."

"Who's running the case?"

"Carl and agent Luke Thorpe will head the investigation."

"Luke's a rookie, and this perp's bad news."

"I understand that. But Luke and Carl deserve a chance to prove themselves."

"C'mon, Cole. Put me on it. I'll take my vacation later."

"No. You're still reeling from that shooting a month ago. You need a vacation."

Cole was right. Going on the cruise would be the closest thing to a vacation that Ross had had in years. Ross shifted his weight awkwardly from one foot to the other and frowned with concentration. A mental picture of Carol's mutilated body kept appearing before his eyes. His posture seemed to stiffen. "I have dreams about guys like this. Bad dreams."

Cole folded his arms across his chest and then leaned back against the plush leather. "But you're still on the case until I leave my office today. Is that clear?"

Ross gave the captain an obligatory nod.

"And, anyway, you have to spend time with that daughter of yours. They grow up too fast."

Ross snapped back with a crisp, "Yes, sir!"

He vanished out of the office door without saying another word.

# CHAPTER 8

RACHEL TOLAR WAS A nervous wreck. She kept looking at the bedroom door where Derek was still sleeping. How long would it be before the police found Carol's killer? She knew for fact that Carol didn't have enemies and that the killing probably wasn't random. It seemed too personal. It might be all Rachel's fault. And the killer might be coming after her. That idea frightened Rachel. A lot.

Flopping on a couch, she switched on the TV, trying to get her mind off the horror of what had happened. But the only thing that engaged her interest was Carol's murder. Her heart, like that of a bird sensing capture, raced with unfamiliar fear. Carol's death brought all the memories rushing back. Her past was coming back to haunt her, and it was the worst feeling in the world. She leaned over the end table, picked up a book, and removed a picture of her, Isabelle, Carol, and Kathy standing together in the lounge of a cruise ship. Rachel recalled being with Carol as they sat in Rachel's attorney's office three years earlier.

"You know it's a lie," Rachel said.

Carol said, "You don't know that for sure. After all, the fairness of our judicial system is based solely on whether the truth is told in court."

But now Carol was dead.

Unable to resist, Rachel bolted across the living room and scurried into the bedroom. "Honey, wake up."

Derek mumbled sleepily, "What is it?"

"Carol's dead."

Derek's eyes bulged, mouth open in complete and total surprise. "Carol's what?"

"She's dead. Someone killed her. And I'm the one that found her."

Derek jumped to his feet. "J-Jesus," he said, pounding one fist into the other palm. "Bastard. Why Carol?"

"Who knows? He might have an obsession about overly fat women. But you know something?" she added suddenly. "We're still going on that cruise. I wanna be away until that killer's found. He might want me next."

Surprise spilled out from Derek's voice. "Gee, babe, you're not." He couldn't bring himself to finish the sentence.

She nodded and whispered the missing word. "Serious."

"Why you? You're not an overly fat woman."

"Regardless, he might have seen me going in or coming out of Carol's house. And he might even have followed me home."

Derek buried his face in his hands.

And Rachel's suppressed memories started flooding back.

Three years earlier, Rachel Tolar remembered being a passenger aboard M/S *Satisfaction*, the flag vessel of Saturn Cruise Lines. She recalled her waiter, Mario Silva. "My name is Silva. Mario Silva. I can get you anything or anyone."

By then Rachel had already pioneered the world of cruising, which had become the fastest growing sector of American leisure, beating leisure resorts, theme parks, and excursions. And it seemed suddenly that people from Florida to Florence who had never left their hometown or rural communities were finding themselves on a cruise ship, all in the pursuit of having fun. From the introduction on, Rachel was captivated by Mario's charm. "I want you to experience the freedom and the hospitality that the ship has to offer," he advised Rachel. "Do what you want and forget about the guilt. Every temptation in abundance and no secrets leave the ship."

Rachel's friends, Carol, Isabelle, and Kathy, who would later be called as witnesses at the trial to help put Rick Solomon away, didn't like Mario Silva too much. He was always coming on to Rachel. He did prove to be the best waiter they had ever had since they began going on cruises. Mario was a rule bender, a macho man full of charm. On virtually every cruise, he took girls down to his room. His balls were aching for Rachel the minute he'd laid eyes on her. He was such a charmer that he had captured Rachel's heart in a matter of two days.

Opening his door to let the female passengers go back to their cabins was always the moment of truth. What if a security guard was watching him or following the girls? What if the staff captain found and asked: "Why is a female passenger in your room?" What if he was caught? Impossible. Absolutely impossible. Silva was far too prudent. Too careful. Too slick. And in the unlikely event he did get caught, he probably would have been given a second chance because he was, without a doubt, the best waiter on the ship. And everyone knew it.

"I should have turned in with my friends or at least had another drink for this journey," Rachel said to Mario as they walked through the hallway and down some stairs.

Mario smiled. "Let your waiter take care of this. Didn't your friends want to come? This party's been planned for three days."

"They're not party animals like me."

Mario smiled again as they passed a sign that read: Crew Only—Passengers Prohibited. "Well, at least we got the best of the bunch, don't we?"

He looked both ways, slid the fire door open, and let Rachel slip through. "And besides, my *paisanos* want to meet you."

"Well, I guarantee to entertain."

"I'm sure you will."

Salsa could be heard from down the hall.

"Are there a lot of people down there?"

"More than you can handle."

When Rachel walked into Mario's cabin, there were about six or seven crew members and a younger woman. The men watched her enter. To Rachel's surprise, Mario claimed the woman's hand. "I have to go."

"But we just got here."

Mario moved closer to Rachel. "Anita needs a little something extra that only I can deliver." He pinched his fingers in front of his nose. "And I have something I want to give her."

A sly look appeared on Mario. "But don't worry, my *compadres* here will go out of their way to take care of you."

"But I don't know them."

"They don't know you, either. But that's not going to stop the fun. And most of them will be gone after tomorrow, anyway."

"So just lay back," he reassured her. "Have a drink and do what you do best. After all, this party is yours."

He slapped Rachel's butt and left with Anita.

As booze flowed, Rachel relaxed. Then her nightmare began when she entered the bathroom and dropped her panties. The minute she sat on the toilet, the lights went out as if they were timed. "Mario," she said as the door opened and someone stepped in. "Is that you?"

But when the lights came back on, Rachel was being held against the wall by a crew member holding a knife. "Scream and you die." His eyes were as dark as Texas oil. He was missing a tooth right on the fifty-yard line.

Her luck! Rachel tussled, "What are you doing?" The man started ripping her dress. "What do you want?"

"I want you," he shot back. "That's what I want."

"Let go of me."

Even to her ears, her demand sounded pretty weak and dizzy. But pretty weak and dizzy was how she felt.

"And if you make another sound and disobey," said the man, putting a hand on her throat and squeezing softly, "I swear you won't get out of here alive."

Incredulity showed on her face, anguish in her eyes.

"Please don't do this to me. I beg you," she said, fighting back tears.

The man ignored her plea, forced his hand down between her breasts, and then down on her privates. Rachel put both of her hands on his, tried to pull away. Couldn't. He was strong. "Let go of me, please."

The aroused man didn't reply. He forcefully pried her legs open, shoved his erect penis inside her, and started pounding against her like an angry shore sailor. Rachel felt increasingly numb, sickened almost to the point of vomiting. She wanted to bolt out of the bathroom door and run like hell. But she was being squeezed against the wall, the commode on her right, the tiny sink on her left. Nowhere to run. When the man finally broke loose, she thought she was going to pass out. But the pain and terror kept her awake. The assailant zipped up and walked out of the bathroom. Rachel tried to put herself back together. But as she proceeded to open the door, another man barged in, blocking her escape. Then another man raped her. And another.

By the time Rachel managed to make a run for the front door, she was in terrible pain, and she felt excruciatingly sick. Staggering through the corridor, she saw no one. And she had no idea where she was. *Lord,* she thought, *show me the way to my room. Don't let me pass out. Please send someone to my rescue.*

But as she followed a corridor leading up to a narrow stairway, her terror turned into relief as Rick Solomon ran to her assistance. "Are you okay, ma'am?" he asked.

Rachel's head throbbed. Under her breath, she said, "Please, help me find my cabin." The words still echoed in her memory.

"Where's your cabin? Oh, my God, you're bleeding! What happened to you?"

Rachel passed out. When she regained consciousness, she found out that Rick Solomon was accused of her rape, even though she knew that he was only trying to help her. But for some reason she decided against it.

When the ship arrived in Miami the next morning, the ship's officials turned the case over to the authorities. Rachel got off the ship, emotionally sick and beaten, and went straight to the hospital. Rick Solomon was taken into custody on shore. And Mario got away with it all.

Carol's lawyer, Mike Bird, paid Rachel a visit. "Would you be willing to press charges against Rick? We ... I mean you," he said correcting himself, "could sue the cruise lines for millions."

"I don't think he was one of them."

"But how do you know?" retorted the conniving attorney. "You were drunk. And it was dark down there."

"I don't know, Mike."

"Look, I'm willing to go to bat for you."

Carol interjected. "Rachel, listen to Mike, will you?"

"According to the report," Mike said, reading a note to her, "Rick Solomon was seen with you when you lost consciousness. He's one of them."

"I'm so confused, Mike."

Mike Bird stared at Rachel gravely, edged closer to the bed, and said, "Listen to me. I know it's confusing, but the bottom line is the cruise ship staff has done you wrong, and you should make them pay. Rachel," he continued, adjusting his glasses, "the girls are willing to testify against him. You know that, don't you?"

"But."

"No buts," argued Mike. "Think about your situation for a second. You've got no money, no medical insurance, no immediate family. How are you going to pay your bills?"

Rachel said nothing. And he moved in for the kill. "Now, for the last time. Do you want me to proceed with the paperwork or not?" He wanted her to agree more than he had ever wanted anything else.

Convinced, Rachel said, "Okay."

"Now," said Mike, pulling out the lawsuit from his briefcase and sliding a legal pad under the contract so the signing would be smoother, "if you're willing to do this, you're going to do it all the way. Nothing half-assed. Is that clear?"

"Yes."

He uncapped a pen and then made her sign the contract.

Then came the trial. As agreed, Isabelle Palmer and Carol Bolton took the stand and testified against Rick. He was sent to prison for doing nothing wrong. And, of course, Rachel sued for a ton of money.

Over the past three years, this incident had been the biggest secret of Rachel's life. Not even Derek knew about it. Shame had always silenced her. When Derek asked her about her financial stability, she confided in him that she'd inherited lots of money from her grandfather. But now she felt like she must speak out and tell somebody what had happened. The unreasonable reality was that if Rick had been set free, based on Carol's explicit torture and death, he could be systematically killing everyone who'd testified against him. She could be next.

Rachel Tolar was trapped between a rock and a hard place.

Derek woke Rachel from her uneasy nap. "Honey, wake up."

For a moment, Rachel did not know whether she was at home or on the ship. Derek gave her a strange look as she quickly focused on his face.

"There are two men here to see you."

An hour earlier, Carl and Ross were on their way to see Rachel. Carl followed Ross to the parking lot and then said, "Shouldn't we call her first? I mean she might not be home, right?"

Ross yanked open the door of his Mustang and got behind the wheel. "She's home. I'm sure of it."

They drove to Interstate 95 on Grandon Boulevard and pulled into a luxurious apartment building called Bel-Air. They were greeted by green lawns, exotic plants all around, and the general appearance of the estate was one of space, luxury, and absolute tranquility.

"What a place!" exhaled Carl as they stood in the entryway of the living room. "Some folks certainly know how to live, don't they?"

"No shit."

"How can she afford a place like this?" asked Carl. "These joints must run a fortune."

"Did you ask her who pays her rent?"

Just then Rachel entered wearing a long-sleeve denim shirt with the word kaleidoscope embroidered in fancy pink script across her left pocket. "Gentlemen, I'm sorry," she said with a straight face. Tears stood in her eyes but didn't fall. "The events of the day were too much for me."

Ross said, "We were nearby and thought we'd drop by."

"Please make yourselves comfortable," she said, waving them to a couch.

Carl said, "We probably should have called—"

"No, it's okay."

The detectives sat down. "Whew!" Carl whistled, looking around the apartment. "Very nice place you've got here, Rachel."

Rachel's apartment was like a model home. Expensive paintings hung on every wall. The living room was furnished with white crushed-velvet couches and chairs. The carpet was white with gold flecks. A refrigerator for the wet bar was cleverly disguised as part of the wall. A separate large snack bar separated the den from the kitchen. From where they sat, Carl could see a telescope mounted on the balcony, which overlooked the ocean. The view of Key Biscayne was spectacular.

"Thank you," Rachel said.

"Nice shirt. What is Kaleidoscope?" Ross asked.

"It's a new nightclub in South Beach. Derek's father owns it."

The detectives glanced at each other. "Umm, I guess Ross and I need to check it out."

"Sure," Rachel said. "Gentlemen, what can I do for you?"

"Need some more questions answered," Ross said. "And the first is what do you do for a living?"

"Are these questions about Carol or me?"

Ross said, "Never know which direction an investigation will take."

"Well, if you need to know, I don't work."

Ross said bluntly, "You a kept woman?"

Rachel laughed. "I have no problem using men. But there's more ways besides a man or a job to make money."

Carl guessed, "A lawsuit?"

A startled Rachel replied, "Can't disclose!"

Carl and Ross exchanged glances again. As he chewed on Rachel's statement, Ross said, "So, how long have you known Ms. Bolton?"

"About five years."

"Do you know her parents?"

"No."

"How well did you know her?"

Rachel's voice shook, as if she might begin to cry again. Carl wanted to reach out and squeeze her hand reassuringly. He understood what she was going through.

"She is one of my best friends."

Carl understood why she said she is instead of she was. Lots of people did that after someone close to them died suddenly.

Ross said, "And you said earlier that there appeared to be nothing missing?"

"Why is that important?"

"Because we believe that this murder is personal. Do you have any idea of what it might be?"

"Being in the wrong place at the wrong time."

Ross said, "Why were you there this morning?"

Rachel looked at Carl. "Like I told him. She wouldn't return my calls, and I began to worry."

Ross nodded. "I see."

Carl noticed more tears as Rachel reached out for a Kleenex on the coffee table and wiped her teary eyes. He asked, "Did she ever receive any threatening letters?"

"No."

"Did anyone ever stalk or follow her?"

She shook her head to indicate she had no idea.

"Was she dating anyone?"

"No."

"Ever?" added Ross quickly.

Rachel shook her head. "No."

Carl looked at her uncomprehendingly. "You mean she never had a boyfriend in her whole life?"

"How am I supposed to know?"

"I'm sorry," Carl said. "We have to ask."

"Had she ever been involved in a car accident?" asked Ross. "We noticed a wrecked car on the lawn."

"Yes."

"How long ago?"

"A couple of months or so."

"Was she in the right or wrong?"

"She blew a Stop sign."

Carl frowned. "Was she drunk?"

"Yes."

"My apologies for having to ask this," Ross said. "You were one of her best friends. Again, try to understand me. We all have flaws. We were born with them. I personally have lots of them. And I'm not proud. Was she an alcoholic?"

Rachel made a face. "An alcoholic?"

Ross said, "Well ..."

"No. She was not an alcoholic," Rachel said. "Anything else?"

"How can we reach this Isabelle?" Carl said, seeing goose bumps on her arms where the sleeves of her shirt had slid back.

"She went to Jacksonville this morning to stay with her sister. I don't have her sister's number."

Ross said, "If she calls you, call us."

"I will, as long as you remember that it's Carol that's dead. Not me or Isabelle."

They shook hands with Rachel and left.

Closing the door behind them, Rachel couldn't bring herself to explain why she hadn't told them everything. She had been worried that they would think less of her. She knew she must speak up. Already she felt the responsibilities piling on her conscience. Terrified by the impending danger, Rachel burst into an agonized cry and forced herself to sleep.

As Rachel dozed off, a disappointed Derek flopped on a couch and remembered one of the fondest memories of his adulthood. He had met Rachel a year ago during the annual Lipton tennis championship final in Key Biscayne, Florida, and between a changeover, he had dropped into the vacant seat next to her. He was the type of player who wasted no time. "No offense, but your eyes are driving me loco, pretty lady," he said, calling the shots, sounding like the perfect gentleman.

"None taken."

He stared deeply into her eyes and considered Rachel's beauty, finding her exquisite. Her body was truly sensational. "What's your name?" he asked.

"Rachel Tolar."

"I'm Derek Smalls," he said. "I'm very delighted to meet you, Rachel."

"Likewise."

"Are you here all alone?" he said, his body tangling with anticipation.

"Well ..." Rachel hesitated, as if reluctant to proceed. "You could say that."

"Would you like to go out with me for dinner, lunch maybe, or even breakfast?"

Rachel giggled, beautiful teeth flashing. Her expensive, clean feminine smell invaded his nostrils. "You wanna go out with me?" Her voice was soft like a river running dry.

"I promise you. I won't bite."

"Just so you know. I'm every bit as tough as I'm attractive."

"Then I will send you flowers once a week, cards just about every week, chocolates whenever it rains, and champagne whenever it doesn't—until you melt."

A slow smile spread across her face. It was not conveyed solely by the curve of her luscious lips. Her eyes were a part of it, too—so clear, so blue, filled with what seemed to be pure affection. "But I don't know you."

The tennis match resumed. Pete Sampras served his third ace to MaliVai Washington, and the spectators let out a roar. Derek whispered. "You do now."

From that day onward, they remained in a state of bliss, almost inseparable. Togetherness was the name of the game. Rachel proved to be smart, outgoing, understanding, and genuinely honest. He hadn't encountered these qualities in any of his ex-girlfriends. And, she was down-to-earth simple. But after listening to Rachel's gruesome testimony, he could reach one inescapable conclusion: What he thought he knew about Rachel was either wrong or incomplete.

# CHAPTER 9

AT A PAY PHONE, Rick Solomon found a listing for Isabelle Palmer. She wasn't home. Isabelle lived in a duplex in Miami overlooking a park near the fairgrounds. There were cars parked on either side of the street. A softball game was in progress. Rick parked the minivan on a grassy incline, fifteen yards from Isabelle's door. He walked into the park and sat on a wooden bench. It was nearing eight o'clock, and the evening air was still warm. A breeze had sprung up from the northeast.

Watching a kid crush a pitch jogged Rick's childhood memories. Images of Gus playing softball kept appearing before his eyes. He remembered how Gus had been as a child—brave and adventurous, fluid and intense, and unafraid of danger. He excelled at the game so much that once he was at the plate, he'd crush the pitches, sending them well over the fence, completely out of sight. At one point, not only could Rick see Gus in his mind, but he could also hear him say, "Raise the bat higher, higher! Hit the ball hard!" The memory played before his eyes as if he were watching it on a movie screen. "Run, run, run!" And then the crowd let out a roar after a home run on the softball field, snapping him out of the reverie.

At ten o'clock, the softball game was over. Soon the park was closed, and darkness fell over the sidewalk where he was parked. He sat in his car watching Isabelle's door for hours, waiting for her to come home. He intended to wait for her all night if need be. After all, he was in no particular hurry. He'd get her. He knew it was only a matter of time. *Yes,* he thought. *I'll get the bitch.*

At 2:00 AM, he saw a woman pull a silver Toyota Camry into the driveway assigned to Isabelle's duplex. A late-model Nissan 240ZX angled in beside her. The woman was Isabelle Palmer. Unquestionably, she was one of the three women who had testified against him. The driver of the Nissan was a tall, athletic black man who looked like Mike Tyson. His T-shirt flexed with pure muscle. Rick watched, his pulse rate quickening, as they held hands and went inside the house. The minutes stretched into hours. The radio was tuned to a contemporary music station. Gloria Estefan sang about always tomorrow, and Rick was fascinated by the way in which things connected briefly. But the irony was Rick wanted to confront the bitch now. Not tomorrow. Not the next day. But now. Irritably, he changed station.

At four-thirty in the morning, his determination paid off. He saw Isabelle leave her house and put her arms around the black man, who popped the trunk and shoved a suitcase in her car. Rick's mind was in a whirl. Did she realize she was next? Isabelle and the black man kissed. Isabelle got into her Camry, started the engine, belted herself in, and reversed out of the parking space. The black man followed. Rick waited a few seconds before slipping into traffic behind them. They drove onto Sixth Avenue and then pulled into an Amoco gas station at the intersection of 125th Street and West Dixie Highway. Rick saw the black man go inside the convenience store, and then he returned to fuel Isabelle's car. He walked up to the driver's side window and gave her a passionate kiss, and they both left in opposite directions.

Rick smiled. *Bitch's going somewhere. On her own.*

Leaving the Amoco gas station, the Camry headed west. At the intersection of 125th Street and Sixth Avenue, it turned right and zoomed up a ramp onto Interstate 95. As Rick followed, he removed the sound suppressor from the console and screwed it onto his .32-caliber pistol. Isabelle left Interstate 95 and entered the Florida Turnpike, heading north, and proceeded through the toll plaza.

Rick sped after the Camry on the deserted turnpike. There was road construction ahead and a no passing lane. The two-lane highway was becoming narrower. He kept fingering the weapon as he moved closer. With the speedometer registering ninety miles an hour, Rick thought this was exciting. He was now half a mile from her. Then, as he passed a sign announcing the entrance to Palm Beach County, he noticed in the rearview mirror an eighteen-wheeler barreling down on him, closing in fast. Rick stepped harder on the accelerator, desperately trying to catch not only Isabelle, but also to get some distance between him and the truck. If not, the truck was surely going to slam into his minivan and run right over him.

"Motherfucker," he said loudly.

Isabelle listened to the radio as she wheeled the Camry skillfully onto the turnpike. The pines on both sides were tall and dark, flashing past in a blur. The sky was powdered with stars and only marred by one strip of white cloud. At eighty-five miles per hour, the engine was almost silent. The tires hummed pleasantly on the well-surfaced pavement. At this early morning hour, the flat highway was deserted, and no traffic was in sight for miles. As she fiddled with the air-conditioning controls, a motorcycle hurtled by on the opposite side of the road, going to unknown destination. It was the first traffic she had seen.

From the rearview mirror, Isabelle saw a minivan catching up. She sped up. Instantly, her breathing quickened. Her frantic, rattling heart was pounding against the walls of her chest, shaking her to pieces. To Isabelle Palmer, the danger was no small thing. Her acquaintance with the mystery of death was brief and vivid. Her mind blazed with questions.

*Am I being followed? If so, by whom and why? But no one has a grudge against me. No one should be following me. No one has a legitimate reason to follow me! Certainly not at this hour!*

The thoughts generated in her an apparent sense of safety. As she looked back in the rearview mirror, an eighteen-wheeler followed behind the minivan that was approaching fast. On the radio, a newscaster gave the weather forecast: "It's going to be a beautiful day, folks." Isabelle observed the unseen driver of the minivan flashing his headlights, and she added to the announcer's commentary: "By being safe now!"

Without another second of hesitation, she jammed hard on the gas pedal to get some distance between the two cars, until she noticed the eighteen-wheeler practically pushing the minivan along. The Camry sped forward, opening a small gap between her and the minivan. The speedometer climbed to one hundred and then up to 105 miles per hour. The steering wheel vibrated in her hands. Shaken, she tried to steer over to the right, where the shoulder widened so the two vehicles could pass. Then a look of horror appeared on Isabelle's face as the driver in the minivan aimed a pistol at her. Fear bubbled darkly within Isabelle. Her heart was now thundering in her chest, and her breathing was roaring in her ears.

As luck would have it, the man missed her. But her front tire exploded as the minivan raced by. The Camry swerved violently, and the truck following too close slammed into the rear bumper. The impact sent the Camry out of control. It overturned, flipped twice, and then crashed into the median strip before coming to a stop.

Rick Solomon smiled as he watched the devastation from the side of the road. He shifted the minivan into reverse, backed up to where the car had overturned, and left the engine running.

With weapon in hand, Rick stood over the truck driver. He was stone-cold dead. No pulse. No movement. No nothing. Then he looked over the Camry in the fading light to see a bloody Isabelle limping away from the wreckage. "You think you can outrun me, you little slut? Not even in your after life."

Rick pointed the weapon and pulled the trigger. The shot pulverized the back of Isabelle's leg. She fell to the ground but staggered back up and started screaming. "Somebody, please help me!" She was shaking like an old car whose engine was badly out of tune; her hair was matted with blood.

Rick laughed at the irony of her plea. "Who's going to help you? The grass, the trees, the sky, God, or me?"

"P-p-please," implored Isabelle, "don't kill me."

But Rick grabbed her hair and knocked her back down. Then he tore a piece of paper from his notebook. "Did you ever consider the consequences of your actions?"

Through chattering teeth, Isabelle managed to say, "W-w-what actions?"

"Hold this!" ordered Rick.

Isabelle quickly obeyed as she took the paper. Rick said, "You don't remember me?"

But then Isabelle was silent as she seemed to remember what she had tried so hard to forget. Rick squeezed her hand together, enveloping the paper in one hand as he slid out his knife with the other. "When you wallow with pigs, expect to get dirty."

Isabelle's angelic face would never look the same again.


Under a flat and gray sky, sunlight was changing to dark. Though rain had not begun to fall, the air seemed tense in expectation of it. Carl left the police station feeling empty, husked out. All afternoon he had piddled around the office replaying Carol's murder. He drove on Biscayne Boulevard in a fog, almost rear-ending a BMW. At a stoplight, he spotted a 7-Eleven, looked at his pager, placed it on the seat by his cell phone, and then made a U-turn. He walked up to the telephone booth. It was now windy. People came in and out of the 7-Eleven in a hurry, their heads tucked down. He jammed his hand into his pocket, fished out a quarter, stepped into the open booth, dropped the quarter in the slot, and dialed the number.

Kim answered the phone on the first ring. "Carl, is that you, darling?"

"Yeah. Let your dad hear that, and he will cut my balls off."

Kim said, "He doesn't know it's you. And I've been calling you all day."

"Yes it's me, Kim. What's up? Why were you calling me?"

"I'm sitting in my bed with my peek-a-boo panties on, and I didn't make the drop."

Carl was upset, though he could almost see her standing there, her young limbs half-exposed.

"Quit that, will you? Why didn't you make the drop?"

"Because somebody else might have picked it up."

"Then give him a call."

"He was on a pay phone."

"Well, you're going to have to wait till he calls you back."

"He won't be able to."

"Why not?"

"I changed my number."

Carl was really angry with her. "Why didn't you tell me that this morning?"

"Because you were in a hurry."

Carl sighed. "Anything else you want to tell me?"

"Oh, I put the credit card number on your answering machine. The number from the card that was in the bag I dropped. I also gave you the address of the mailbox."

With a bit of sarcasm in his voice, Carl said, "I'm glad the mailbox has an address. It just means the more trouble I'll get into when it all comes out."

Unconcerned, Kim said, "And there was an envelope in the parcel as well that I didn't open."

"Well, there's nothing we can do about it, is there?"

"And guess what?"

The rain was pouring on Carl. He said with even more sarcasm, "I'm getting soaked while I'm losing my career."

"I'm going to miss you so much."

"You're only gone for four days and you're back."

Deep sincerity entered her voice. "But be safe, okay?"

"I will, Kim," he said, just as she wanted him to say.

Carl hung up the phone. He was beginning to wish he had never moved to South Florida.

# CHAPTER 10

AT HOME, RICK SOLOMON was brimming with a sense of glory and victory. He was on a roll, doing far better than he had anticipated. Within only twenty-four hours of his release, his mission was almost accomplished. What a leap!

From his bag, he took out the newspaper clipping, folded it in half, walked over to the trash can, and threw the clip away. Smiling, he took the old faded pillow and stuffed it into the trashcan, too. Then he turned his attention to the C.I.R on the ceiling. "Two sluts down and one to go." He laughed and said, "What am I going to do with the rest of my life?" He picked up a marker from the table. "But that's not right," he said, adding the letter K for Kim. "It's two sluts down and *two* to go."

When Rick found her, he would knock her naughty ass off the ground, shatter her insolence, and then teach her a lesson that would stick forever. As he marveled at his scribbling on the ceiling, Rick made a startling discovery.

*That's my name up there! My name!*

Rick was a man with relatively few vices. Raised by his grandmother, Martha Martino, a devout Christian, as a young teenager Rick was shy, clumsy, and horrified of puberty. He didn't smoke or drink. He was not judgmental of others and was never affected by what people thought of him. "He was a very lonely man, always deep in thought," said one of his cabinmates. "And hard to know like a closed book."

And reading books was his hobby—the only one. Rick didn't watch TV too much, not that he had anything against it. But what he didn't like about it was the way it turned him away from the rest of the world and to nothing but its own glassy self. In that one way, at least radio was better. Unlike his brother, Gus, he was as good as his word, totally stable, always straight as an arrow, always apologizing when wrong. "To apologize when wrong," he'd say, "is a sign of maturity and draws respect. Although it may not seem so at the time."

Unlike Gus who thought women were nothing but disposable objects, Rick was always considerate of women. Never yelled at them. Never hit them. He had always been respectful of them, and of any authority figure, like Granny. And, since some mendicants became homeless by no fault of their own, Rick had always shown a precocious maturity and sense of compassion for less-fortunate souls and the genuinely victimized. By all accounts, Rick wasn't just a gentleman, but a *damned good* gentleman.

At twenty-nine, Rick's intimate relationships with women totaled exactly three. In each case, Rick enjoyed the lovemaking immensely. He was strictly a one-woman man. To a woman whom he loved, Rick gave her his body, mind, and soul, and he trusted her without reserve. But he had a big problem. Rick simply had no natural inclination for sex; having sex was a trait he still had to acquire. Hence, for the past ten years, he had been alone.

But Rick's time in prison changed all that, changed him deeply, robbing him of his natural kindness and respect for others. In prison, he became a different man, a man who was convinced that the greater portion of the human race was purely animal. And if nothing else, it was in prison that he learned about himself, about the true person he was.

Rick's first days in prison were the hardest. He felt his whole life was blown away in a blink of an eye, with nothing left but all the time in the world to think about it. Each night he would go to bed with a burst of intense anger at Rachel Tolar and her friends, at the whole system that had railroaded him, despite his innocence. *When I get out,* he promised himself, *I will give Rachel hell. That lying, thoughtless bitch—*

Rick shaved and showered. When he was finished, he toweled himself off, brushed his teeth, hand-washed the sink, and burned some rosemary oil that stimulated his mind and body. Rosemary oil was said to improve the memory and give clarity of thought. Then he stretched out on his bed, a soft mattress for the first time in three years, and breathed the privilege of freedom. He smiled, remembering Gus telling him, *"Nothing in this world is free. Not even freedom."* Staring at the ceiling, time was lost to him as he recalled some of the most horrible days of his life before going to prison. The court scene was still frozen in his memory like a photograph—the trial, the jury, the witnesses, the media, and then the DNA evidence that had set him free.

Rick forced himself to smile at the memories. Through the window, a sycamore smiled in the sun, the fall sky was blue and bright, and the sun was shining. The hot morning drowsed by. He closed his eyes and fell asleep. He slept for ten hours and woke up feeling new, fresh, fantastic, energetic, and immaculate, as if he had just been reborn. Almost everything had fallen into position perfectly. And the speed at which things were happening had him dazzled. He got out of bed.

Out the window, it was now dark. The digital clock put the time at 10:20 PM.

Rick squeezed into a blue blazer and a pair of khaki slacks with a braided belt. He put on his dark shades and stared at his reflection in the mirror. He was fascinated by what he saw. Robert De Niro in the flesh. The stance, the eyes, the height, the scar that could be mistaken for De Niro's birthmark. Not quite Robert De Niro, but he was on his way. While he was in prison, he'd watched several of De Niro's films over and over, especially *Cape Fear*, and he was convinced that he and De Niro had something in common. One day he would make De Niro proud. De Niro was a man who understood the process of getting even. In that respect, Rick figured he was the same as De Niro.

Saturday night in South Beach was a riot. And the Kaleidoscope was certainly the kind of place that did good business on the weekend. From a distance, you could see that the club was happening. A large neon sign was set atop a two-story building, and huge floodlights slanted directly above the sign. The beams of the spotlights shone down upon the yellow and green lettering of the neon sign. Outside, the grounds of the club were spotless. It looked as if the club had been painted last week. Valet parking attendants were running this way and that, as if they were mechanical mice. People waited impatiently in line to get in. A typical Saturday night.

Rick parked the minivan in a no-parking zone across from the nightclub. He dodged a spike-haired dude trying to read his palm. "I live in the moment," the dude barked. A slight chill from the ocean bit the night air as Rick dashed across the street. He tipped the doorman a twenty. Rick didn't want to stand in line, and a tip would get him into the nightclub with no waiting. At the front door was a pretty blonde wearing cutoffs. She had eyes as brown as Rick's. She ushered him in with a megawatt smile. On her left breast was a button with her name written in fancy script: Rose. And just below that was a lively greeting: You're Special! "Enjoy your evening, sir," cooed the girl warmly. Her voice was a definite turn-on.

Inside the Kaleidoscope was a madhouse. The dance floor was lit and animated by the latest light and sound system technology. Multicolored laser beams blinked and swept over the crowd. One hundred fifty or two hundred people, mostly between twenty and thirty, but some as young as sixteen, were screaming or dancing to booming rap. Rick surveyed the club with an expert eye before he found a barstool at the bar. A burly bartender approached him.

"Can I get you anything?" the bartender asked.

Rick said, "No. Not unless you're Sean Elmore."

The bartender scowled, his lips twisting in a sneer. "You're early and he's late. Who's asking?"

Rick said, "An old friend."

"And you never knew your friend was black?"

Rick curbed a wild impulse to stomp on the bartender's face. "I'll be back when he's here."

Leaving the bar, Rick looked forward to taking in the fresh evening air. But as he reached the exit, he saw revolving red lights flashing outdoors and a cop with a notepad roaming around the minivan. Rick turned from the door and looked back at the bar. He was arguing with himself. *Maybe the law is closing in on me. Somehow they've found out I'm the one who murdered Carol and Isabelle, even though I have been extremely watchful.* Rick scowled. He wouldn't let them put the handcuffs back on him. No way. Once was enough. Now he would resist. Thrusting his hand into his blazer pocket, he clicked back the safety of his .32-caliber pistol and waited for the cop to come in after him. He would turn around slowly and spray him with bullets. But he relaxed his grip on the weapon when he noticed the cop get back in his sedan and then drive off.

A short time later, Rick was sitting at the bar nursing a Coke when a black man appeared behind the bar. "You Sean?"

"That's my name."

"Have you seen Rachel come in tonight?"

Sean didn't hear him. "Excuse me. Who?"

Rick repeated, "Rachel."

Sean looked at him, obviously suspicious. It was hard to tell if Sean was thirty or forty. His dark hair was heavily oiled and pulled tightly into a knot. His face was thin and clean. It was also difficult for Rick to tell if Sean's head was extra large or his body was undersized, but the two didn't fit.

"Who wants to know?" Sean asked.

"Gus's little brother, Rick."

Sean grinned. "Yeah, man. I should have known. There's not an ice cube colder than you two look. And I'll tell you the same thing I told Augustus. She's taken. And my boss, Derek, is going to make her an honest woman this weekend."

Rick feigned surprise. "You mean hitched. And I wasn't invited?"

"Everyone's invited if they can afford the cruise."

"Which cruise?"

Sean said, "You didn't hear M/S *Redemption* from my mouth."

Rick slapped hands with Sean and was out of there. A parking ticket was wedged between the windshield and the wiper of the minivan. *A fucking damned parking ticket,* Rick thought, tearing the citation up and tossing the pieces away. The gentle breeze carried the tatters across the parking lot.

Rachel awoke on Sunday morning clutching a teddy bear to her chest and softly murmuring Carol's name in the dimly lit bedroom. There was a sour, metallic taste in her mouth. Guilt twisted her, flowed over her like a lava over a town. Her anguish had become so intense that it scraped her nerves raw. Her eyelids felt as heavy as lead. She'd only slept for three hours, and those hours had been plagued by nightmares. Except for the sound of her breathing and the frantic beats of her heart, the apartment was silent. Through the east side curtain, the sun was still just a faint glimmer to the east. The clock put the time at forty-three past five. Her thoughts darted in a thousand directions, not helped any by yesterday, along with today's expectations rising in intensity with each passing minute.

She flicked the night lamp on. Then she rubbed at her itchy eyes with the back of one hand as she looked in the mirror hung on a nearby wall. She saw a disheveled, tired, and confused woman who looked like a parent who's spent too much time with a hyperactive child. The early morning passed quickly, and she did nothing but try to get herself together. At around eleven o'clock, just before she and Derek made ready for their cruise, Rachel picked up Carl's business card, stepped onto the balcony with the portable phone, shut the sliding door behind her, and made the call.

At around the same time on the first floor of the Miami Shores Police Department building, Detective Carl Levy sat at his computer in his office, checking through his notes. His shoulders slumped heavily under the weight of the day. One by one he reevaluated his notes, setting out pieces of the puzzle, twisting and turning them to see where they might fit together. But so far there was no connection. Captain Cole barged in, slid a copy of *Miami Herald* in front of him.

"Can you believe this mess?" Cole growled. "I bet you a million bucks it's the same lunatic who offed yesterday's vic."

"How do you know?"

"He left a note from a notebook denigrating our judicial system and then carved the words *She's sorry* into her face, probably while she was still alive."

"Where did this happen?"

"Read the story. And a truck driver was killed, too."

Carl shook his head. *Just another fucking day in south Florida*, he thought. His cell phone rang.

"You and Luke need to get on the streets. Find this bastard. Now!"

Carl was thoroughly confused, and Cole left him that way. The door slammed, and he could hear Cole growling his way down the hall.

Carl answered his cell. "Hello?"

A woman said, "Detective Carl Levy, please."

"Speaking. Who's calling?"

"Rachel Tolar."

Carl lurched forward and cleared his throat. "Hey, Rachel. I was just thinking about you."

Carl picked up the paper. It featured a dramatic headline: Bizarre Accident and Murder. Carl said, "Hold on just a sec." The lead of the story read: "Truck driver Frank Cuomo, 42, and motorist Isabelle Palmer, 29, were both found dead on the Florida Turnpike yesterday morning. According to investigators, Ms. Palmer was trying to get away from the wreckage when she was brutally murdered. A passerby spotted the accident at 4:45 AM and called the police."

"Hello? Are you still there?" Rachel asked.

"Yeah, I'm here," Carl said. "Sorry. What can I do for you?"

"I've got something to tell you," Rachel said. Her voice sounded garbled, as if she was under water. "Are you with me?"

"Yeah, sure. I'm with you."

"Oh, Carl, I-I'm scared," she said. She sounded confused, bitter, and disappointed. "I don't know if I should tell you this."

"Please, Rachel, talk to me," Carl said. "This is off the record. Way off the record. I promise you."

Rachel said, "I think I know who murdered Carol."

"Oh yeah? Who might that be?"

"His name is Rick Solomon, and Carol helped me put him in prison for raping me. Only he didn't do it."

"Sweet Jesus," Carl said. "You're saying that if Rick is out, he could be responsible for Carol's death?"

"He is Carol's only enemy."

Surprise spilled from Carl's voice as he thought about the other Rick. Carefully, he ticked off details of his conversation with Kim in his head. She said Rick had been in prison and had just gotten out. "He doesn't have a brother by the name of Gus, does he?"

Rachel said, "I don't know."

Carl thought for a moment.

"Carl?" Rachel asked.

"Yeah, I'm here. Just wrapping my mind around this. Listen, Rachel, stay home. I'll put you under police protection."

"That won't be necessary for the next four days. Because I'm going away."

"Away? Where are you going?"

"I'm getting married on the M/S *Redemption* tomorrow night."

Carl scratched his head. "Oh, Lord, Rachel," he said. "Going away right now would not look too good."

"Carl," she said, with genuine misery in her voice, "I didn't mean for this to happen to Carol. I swear. But my fiancé and I had planned this trip a long time ago. Please understand."

Carl could hear Rachel sobbing over the telephone, unable to go on. "It's okay. It's okay, Rachel. I understand. But why didn't you tell me this before?"

"Because I was too confused, too ashamed of what happened to me. Can you imagine what I've been through?"

Something about the way she said it touched Carl deeply. "Look, uh … I'm sorry about the whole thing but …" He considered telling her to call off the wedding plans, but then he changed his mind. "Okay. I'll contact you if I need you before you come back. Oh, by the way," he added, noticing another light on his phone that started to flicker, "did you ever hear from Isabelle?"

"No. Why?"

"No reason. Just wondering. But I have to cut you short. I have got someone else on the other line. So, I'll contact you on the ship."

"Okay. Carl?"

"Yes, Rachel."

"Thanks so much for your understanding. There's a place in heaven for people like you."

Carl took a quivering breath, wondering if letting her go was not going to cost him his career. "Uh, I can hardly wait to get there."

His forefinger cut the connection and then pushed the flashing green light for the next call. "Hello?"

"It's Ross. I'm at the ship terminal. What's happening?"

"It's good you called. I'm going to need you to babysit."

Carl finished up his conversation with Ross and then made a call to City Bank about Rick's credit card. As he was hanging up, Agent Luke Thorpe walked in with a notepad.

"You're right," Thorpe said. "Rick Solomon was released from prison last Friday. His sentence was reduced. He went up for raping our witness Rachel Tolar. Solomon has a brother named Gus who recently died. His grandma lives in Hialeah."

Carl stood up and pushed his chair back. "Then let's roll."

Luke said, "But wait. How did you find out he was a suspect?"

"Rachel just told me."

"Oh shit. If this guy has never been busted on a major felony before, never offed anyone before the rape, hell, not even a traffic violation, I'd say he might be on a major mission."

Carl said, slipping on his jacket, "He's not on a mission. He's at war."

"Where is she?"

"Safely tucked away on a cruise for four days."

"Did Captain Cole approve?"

A shit-eating grin appeared on Carl's face as he closed the door behind Luke. "He didn't say no."

# CHAPTER 11

As the entire Miami police squad was after Rick, he was on the phone with Saturn Cruise Lines, desperately trying to get on M/S *Redemption* in the pursuit of Rachel.

"Thank you for calling Saturn Cruise Lines, where we turn dream vacations into reality," droned a receptionist. "My name is Amy Lewis. How can I help you today?"

Rick said, "Amy, I like your name. Things are sort of pressing in around me, and I was hoping to get away on today's cruise."

"I'm sorry to tell you, but we're fully booked."

"Fully booked?"

Amy said, "We've been fully booked for months, sir."

"For not even one passenger?"

"Sorry."

Rick sighed. It was against his nature to give up. "Amy. Don't let me down. If you can get me on board today, I will always be in your debt."

Amy laughed. Rick pressed on. "Haven't you ever had a day where it seems everyone is after you?"

Silence. Amy said, "Are you local?"

Rick knew he had her. "Certainly."

"I can't promise anything. But if you come to the terminal prior to the end of embarkation and put your name on the stand-by list, they might have a no-show."

Rick said, "Anyone ever tell you that you are what makes the world great?"

Shortly after boarding the ship, Ross and Kim stepped into an elevator and pressed L for the Lido Deck. When the door slid open, the Lido Deck was packed and festooned with balloons, confetti, paper balls, hats, blowers, and the lot. A sea of smiling people of all sizes and shapes milled around. Most were Americans, but virtually every ethnic group was represented. The people lounged against the railings, taking up every inch of space. Around the pool area, teenagers in flowery shirts were dancing or sipping margaritas as a steel band lilted gay rhythms. The passengers were jabbering and flashing pictures as if they had been on a tour excursion. Like Ross, they hadn't expected the ship to be so splendid and heart lifting.

The M/S *Redemption* was a marvel of design and a mastery of engineering. It was dazzlingly conceived and soundly constructed. According the ship's newspaper, the super liner had more innovations than any cruise ship ever built. Strands of neon lights stretched for miles and miles along the deck overlooking the Grand Atrium. Excellent traffic-flow design made for ease in finding the different public rooms and the private cabins. Access to other decks from the lobby was facilitated by two glass-enclosed elevators and elegant staircases curving upward to Atlantic Deck. State-of-the-art lighting and sound systems were featured in the showrooms.

It had taken some fifty design engineers and had cost well over 440 million dollars to bring the ship online. The M/S *Redemption*, a floating palace, had the most modern electronic computer equipment and satellite-run wheelhouse, and enclosed wings that projected well beyond the sides of the ship. Armed with a powerful diesel engine and a two-propeller propulsion system, the ship had a maximum speed of twenty-two knots. It had taken three and a half years to build the ship, equal to about 2.5 million working hours. Forty-one hundred people had been involved in the construction of the ship.

The four-day cruise was to Freeport and Nassau in the Bahamas and offered spectacular botanical gardens, surrey rides, fashionable boutiques, and, to Ross's satisfaction, six of the best golf courses in the tropics. He planned on teeing off on one of them the next morning. As far as entertainment was concerned, there wasn't a show on Broadway that could not find a home in the ship's theater, with its high-tech moving turntable, telescoping wall, and motorized scenery movement. Built in the style of an outdoor amphitheater, three decks high with balconies, the theater seated fifteen hundred people with unobstructed stage views. Additional seating was provided by theater-style cushioned seats on the third floor.

Passengers were greeted by the cruise staff in a spacious reception lobby on the Empress Deck. A book and video library was located on the Atlantic Deck. Public rooms with dominant colors, such as the nightclub, the casino, and the main lounge, were spread out on the Promenade Deck, which was decked out with its sloping floor and super sightlines.

The dining room was definitely one of the best and finest on the seven seas. Ross was impressed. He had to admit it. Table accommodations for any family were guaranteed at all times. And the cuisine? Excellent. Wine, like other drinks, was on the house. Live Maine lobster, caviar, and fresh produce and fruits were served on a daily basis. Artistic presentation was everything. Each plate was prepared individually and became an artistic construction. Passengers were able to dine on the Lido Deck as well as in the restaurants.

The cabins were spacious, carpeted from wall to wall and built with generous closets and comfortable bunks, and securely protected with a high-security system. Each cabin had a TV/VCR system. The cabins ranged in size from four hundred square feet to eight hundred square feet, and were located from the Riviera Deck to the Verandah Deck. And if you happened to be on the Verandah Deck, you experienced full-length bathtubs, queen-size beds, and a minibar.

The entire ship was spacious, cozy, and clean. There were four pools, four bathtubs, and a twisting four-deck-high slide for those seeking a thrill into the pool. All in all, the ship was an extraordinary feat of engineering and the essence of luxury for its passengers.

As Kim busied herself reading the ship's brochure out loud, Ross was preoccupied in thought. He couldn't seem to relax. The memory of yesterday's events consumed him, dancing horrifically before his eyes.

"Listen, Dad. This ship is in the *Guinness Book of Records* as the largest cruise ship passenger ever built!"

Ross was trying to listen, but his mind was back on another boat. Kim continued reading the brochure to him. "The ship can hold three thousand passengers and thirteen hundred crew members. Rising 213 feet above the water at its highest point, the M/S *Redemption* was the first cruise ship too wide to transit the Panama Canal. It is sixty feet taller than the Statue of Liberty, and it stretches nearly three football fields in length, measuring nine hundred feet from bow to stern."

Kim's jaw dropped open as she looked around. Ross laughed. "What were you saying?"

Kim threw the brochure on the nearest table. "Nothing. It's only a book."

Ross became bothered as he watched a woman on a Viking powerboat cruise past the ship. Suddenly, he was overcome by an anxiety attack. Kim also noticed the boat and turned to her father.

"That's not our boat, Dad."

Slightly bitter, Ross said, "That's ridiculous. How could it be ours?"

Kim was looking at him searchingly.

"Ours is at the bottom of the ocean with your mother," he added.

Kim turned away as Ross walked to the railings to catch a fleeting view of the woman and the boat. And the more he stared at the boat, the more his burning sensation grew. Although the atmosphere was festive and very amusing—young girls wearing thongs who were tanning and dancing; young boys who were watching the girls with excited eyes—at each passing moment, Ross was feeling worse. Up above them, the crowds had grown since their arrival. Passengers lined up to take part of the action on the twisting four-deck-high slide, all seeking a thrill into the pool. Riders squealed.

This Memorial Sunday was a scorcher all the way. It was so hot that everybody was squinting. But on top deck, it was merely pleasantly warm with a breeze coming off the water to the east. And if Ross hadn't suffered similar manifestations of shock and intermittent nightmares over the past years, he would have thought that he was losing his mind.

"It's hot, isn't it, Dad?" asked Kim, obviously unaware of his sudden distress.

Ross nodded and managed one word. "Very."

By then he was inconspicuously breathing through his mouth. Unable to resist, he hurried away, seeking refuge in the closest restroom. To his annoyance, the men's room was packed. As he stood in line to get inside, he heard his lost wife, September, scream. It was faint at first, but then the screams became louder. The screams were not the good-humored shrieks of thrill seekers on the twisting four-deck-high slide of the ship, but cries of genuine desperation. He found himself whispering, "*No, no, no, honey! Please don't leave me!*" The line to the men's room moved quickly, and by the time Ross reached one of the sinks in the bathroom to splash cold water on his face, his legs grew weak and his head spun. Ross's sense of burning did not abate. He could feel the bile rising. Abruptly, Ross stormed into the stall, locked the door behind him, and then sat on the toilet.

Inside the restroom was clean and the air was cool, but the pressure on Ross's chest increased. Each hot breath burst from him with a flammable gasp. His stomach contracted into a tight ball. As the seconds and then minutes passed, Ross smelled melting plastic burning. Closing his eyes, the sense of burning intensified. The smell of burning hair and flesh and oil thickened. The scream of September grew louder. Her face kept appearing before his eyes. Ross wanted to puke but couldn't. Smoke engulfed the restroom. The cabin walls. The ceiling. Toxic fumes were filling up his lungs. Hidden tendrils of fire uncoiled like snakes. "Please, Lord," he panted softly. "Help me." Without opening his eyes, he bent double, covering his face with his icy hands, racked by guilt.

Over the years, real and imagined pictures of September in happier times had helped him to cope, had helped him to find his way to one idea after another, pushing the horror of September's fiery death on the boat to the back of his mind and burying it there beneath facts and figures. But this time September's picture did not mesmerize. It wasn't there to comfort him, and he was unable to guide his troubled mind without suffering this latest and worst attack. Like water oozed from the faucet, giving way to the demands of gravity, like gravity demands so much of us that when we rest we fall asleep, like the effect of a planet on its moon, the calendar pulled Ross into its orbit, and he couldn't stop his thoughts from revolving around the date: Memorial Day. It was the seventh anniversary of the boat accident that had crushed him, and the anniversary conjured up memories of his great loss.

The worst had happened to Ross seven years ago to the day, changing his life forever. It had happened on his forty-nine-foot Viking powerboat. The boat was brand spanking new. Its spacious saloon opened to wide side decks and a protected cockpit. Available with a galley-up and two staterooms, the boat offered the comfort of inside steering as well as the superior visibility of a well-equipped flybridge. Armed with a 767-horsepower engine housed in a walk-in engine room, in calm conditions the Viking delivered a cruising speed of thirty knots.

On that fateful Sunday so long ago, Ross, September, and nine-year-old Kim were on the deck of the Viking doing a little deep-sea fishing. The day was gorgeous. The sun was playing hide-and-seek between the clouds. Steady east winds had brought ideal surfing conditions: the offshore fall breezes made near perfect one-to-three-foot waves that peeled off one another with clocklike regularity. Additionally, there was such a vivid happiness in September's eyes that Ross was almost frightened. After only seven months of marriage, not only had she become Ross's inspiration, but she was also his every wonder in the world. At around four o'clock that afternoon, cloud shadows fell over the water. The breeze grew cooler and stronger.

Confused, Kim had said, "How come we went on a picnic before we caught the fish?"

September stood against the railing and smoked a cigarette. "Your dad wanted a picnic before we went deep-sea fishing, and that's good because he might not catch anything."

Ross said, "I heard that. And believe me, you don't want to clean the fish I intend to catch."

Stepmother and Kim snickered at Ross's ineptness as a fisherman. Ross sat there frustrated as September lit another cigarette. She saw dark clouds moving in and said, "Skipper, do you think fish know the difference between good weather and bad?"

Ross retorted, "If we go in now, then you buy dinner."

And suddenly Ross heard an orchestrated reply. "Pizza!"

A short time later, under a rapidly darkening sky, Ross raised the anchor of the boat. And then the unexpected occurred. The engine would not start.

Ross smiled. "I guess we have to wait until we can get a tow truck."

September said, "Not on your life. I could build this engine if I had to."

With a cigarette burning cheerfully in her mouth, her unbreakable habit, September walked down to the walk-in engine room, which was filled with fuel from a leaky fuel line mixed with residual ocean water. As she opened the engine room door, she tripped on the threshold and fell forward. The door closed behind her flailing body. The burning cigarette flew out of her mouth, landed on the fuel-soaked floor, and quickly started a fire that turned the walk-in engine room into a raging inferno. The fire slithered up the wall, mushroomed across the ceiling, and devoured everything combustible in its path. When Ross realized that the boat was on fire, he grabbed a fire extinguisher. As he opened the hatch to the engine room, flames gushed out.

"September!" he screamed. "September! Stay low!"

Although he tried, the flames kept Ross from entering the smoke-filled engine room.

"No, no, don't leave me!" he cried. "Please!" And he started beating on the ceramic door trying to get to September. But it was to no avail. He could still hear her agonized screams. The roar of the fire. And he could still smell that awful smell. The smell of burning flesh and wood and fuel.

Ross opened his eyes and saw the deck he thought he was beating was really the door to a restroom stall. He stopped. As unexpectedly as it came, the horrifying memory passed. Soon he wasn't shaking or sweating anymore, and he was no longer plagued by the sensation of burning. It was gone. The panic and the pain were gone. At least for the time being. Ross opened the door to the stall and found five male passengers standing there staring at him. He didn't apologize. As he exited the restroom, Kim stood there looking very concerned. "Did the man I sent in find you?"

Ross turned and walked away with Kim. "They all did, sweetheart."

As they sat in lounge chairs watching the young men and women scampering around the pool in a primordial mating ritual, Ross noticed a man on the Sports Deck watching the crowd with binoculars. "I guess there are perverts on board ships, too," he mumbled to himself. But he had spoken loudly enough for a cocktail waitress to hear him as she came by. She was carrying a tray of drinks.

"Speaking of perverts," she said. "Would you like a complimentary Sex on the Beach, folks?"

Ross didn't think her joke was funny. She checked with Kim. "Wanna drink?"

Kim nodded approvingly, innocence shining in her eyes. "Please, Dad."

He said, "I'll take two as long as they are not too strong, because my daughter doesn't drink."

The waitress laughed as she shared a knowing look with Kim. Ross was sure to notice. The waitress said, "And I will have a virgin sent to your cabin also, sir."

Kim agreed as she chugged her drink. As the waitress walked away laughing, Ross said, "I guess on a ship you're also allowed to be an ass."

# CHAPTER 12

HEADS TURNED WHEN RACHEL Tolar and her fiancé, Derek Smalls, stepped onto the ship. Two crew members at the purser's office craned their heads to get a good shot of Rachel as she made an unforgettable entrance wearing a crisp white shirt and a windowpane plaid skirt. A black cardigan was draped casually over her shoulders. Chocolate lipstick lent warmth to her mouth. Raven blonde hair combed smoothly back. Riveting blue eyes unreadable beyond darker-than-dark shades. She overheard one crew member say to the other, "Mama mia!" She politely smiled but considered the source.

Minutes later, they were inside their minisuite on the Verandah Deck. Rachel shuddered as she stood solidly in front of the door holding it closed. Derek was more interested in the bed. Snaking his arms around her waist, he rocked her toward him. After a spate of tender hugs and kisses, Rachel seemed more relaxed, more her old self, and she felt a bit calmer. But deep in her heart she knew that the underlying terror that had suddenly emerged in her life would never be over until Rick was captured.

Later, after a walk around the ship, Derek suggested that they take a seat on the Verandah Deck balcony overlooking the main pool area and the Jacuzzi. He watched with quickening pulse as he caught sight of an irresistibly gorgeous blonde clad in a royal blue, daisy-trimmed bikini that exposed far too much bare flesh. She had on Ray-Ban sunglasses. Her lean body was the only thing without a logo. She walked over to a bin, grabbed a towel, and headed in direction of the pool, executing a graceful dive. Then she got out of the pool and settled into a chaise lounge. She rummaged through a duffel bag, extracted an atomizer lotion, and proceeded to spray her gorgeous legs. When she finished, she rolled onto her tummy, eased a finger under the tight elastic of her swimsuit, and fell into a beauty sleep. Derek smiled as Rachel caught him staring. She said, "As long as you don't touch."

With bright, excited eyes, he shot back, "I only have eyes for you, darling."

Rachel reached out and squeezed his hand softly. "And you're a keeper, skipper."


At the counter area of Saturn Cruise Lines, Rick Solomon picked up his ticket and then looked at his watch. "You know what?" he said to the counter person. "I'm not going to have enough time to get my bags."

The representative said, "Here, take this tag. It will show that your bags were checked."

He had stepped on board at five minutes to four, five minutes before the ship set sail. Luckily enough, not only was he allowed a cabin of his own, he was also among the first group of passengers to have their luggage delivered to their staterooms. Rick placed his suitcase on the bed and inspected its contents: nylon rope, knife, sound suppresser, .32-caliber pistol, ammo, and binoculars.

From the bed, he walked into the bathroom and considered his reflection. Satisfied, he extracted a pair of Ray-Ban sunglasses, grabbed his binoculars, and left the cabin. On the Sports Deck, located just above the Verandah Deck, Rick surveyed the sea of people. "C'mon Rachel," he kept saying to himself. "Reveal yourself. Let me share my past with you." For nearly half an hour, he scanned the crowd searching for Rachel Tolar without success. But he was not disturbed by that because if Rachel was on board he knew he would find her.

The last time Rick had seen Rachel in person was the first and last day of the trial. She looked so innocent, so pure, and so frail at the same time. He could vividly remember her saying, "Yes, he was one of the guys who raped me that night." Her big-time lawyer, Mike Bird, pounced on him, told the jury that he was a heartless and dangerous man who deserved to be locked far away from society. Rick, on the other hand, was represented by a public defender named Bart Veino. Rumor had it that Mr. Veino had sat for the bar exam six times before he passed it. He and Rick lost the case on the second hearing.

By 4:30 PM everyone was aboard the ship. Music played, champagne flowed, and the ship's whistle sounded, signaling the departure time, a time that marked the beginning of an exciting journey for Rick. The ship set sail to Freeport, in the beautiful Bahamas. Rick skipped the mandatory lifeboat drill. He knew what to do in the event of an emergency. Instead, he headed down to his room and took a nap. Peaceful minutes went by. Then he was dreaming. In a prison storeroom, Mosby and four other inmates were standing over Rick, who was lying against some barrels partially undressed. One inmate said, "He's had enough."

Mosby displayed his yellow teeth with a vicious smile as the inmates walked away, leaving Rick crying. "Tomorrow's another day, sweetmeat."

A toilet flushed in the next cabin, jarring Rick awake and out of his misery.

After a short drive to Hialeah, Luke and Carl slowly cruised by an abandoned duplex with a racial message spray painted on the walls: Black + White = Hispanic—The Best.

They laughed. Carl saw the address and told Luke to stop.

"What do you mean?"

"I spoke English, right?"

"Right, but we're not there yet."

Carl said, "That's all right. We can see it from here."

Carl got out of the car and stood in front of the abandoned duplex. Even from a distance, there was no indication that the place had been lived in for years. The windows were all broken. The doors were gone and were probably stolen. The grass stood three feet tall. There was no sign of running water or electricity. An old rusty mailbox was located on a post by the gate.

Luke said, "Are we going to go inside this shithole?"

"Nope."

Carl scanned the neighborhood. The street was lined with other duplexes, some of them brownstones, and some brick. Most of them were in bad repair. Bars on the windows indicated breaking and entering was a frequent occurrence. The sidewalk was deserted for the length of the block. From across the street, under the shade of an oak tree, a Hispanic man sat on the hood of an old battered Camaro.

"Then why are we here?" Luke asked.

Carl thought it was too premature to tell Luke that both Rick and Kim had been there. He said, "To ease my mind."

Carl walked over to the Hispanic man. Luke followed right behind Carl.

"Oye, como va?"

"Good."

"You see anyone open that mailbox?" Carl asked.

The Hispanic man was seedy looking and in his midforties. A mole on his chin was the size of a dime. His white T-shirt was emblazoned with the words *Calle Ocho*. His curly long dark hair was tousled. A beer can concealed in a brown paper bag was set on the hood next to him. He looked totally relaxed.

"Si. Yes."

Luke said, "Do you speak English?"

His Spanish accent was heavy. "A little."

Carl showed him the picture of Rick. "Was it this man?"

The man grabbed the picture to take a look. "No. It was a pretty blonde girl."

Luke seemed confused. "Are you sure?"

The man grinned pleasantly, revealing teeth that had had very little acquaintance with a dentist. Nicotine had stained his teeth as yellow as old ivory.

"Yes, a pretty blonde girl."

Luke turned to Carl and pressed, "Pretty blonde girl? Am I missing something?"

Carl said, "I'll explain later. Let's go talk to Rick's grandmother."

They entered through the front gate. Luke was nervous and had his hand on his gun. He walked to the statue. "Howdy, Virgin Mary. Have you seen Rick?"

Carl said, "Shut up. If he's here, I don't want him to think we're morons."

Luke said, "Hey, Jesus. Don't go away, in case we need you."

A nervous Carl rang the doorbell. A dog started barking. "Hello? Anybody home?"

An old woman opened the door slightly. "Just me and my dog. He bites."

Carl said, "Just a quick question, ma'am."

"I do not vote. It doesn't do me any good."

"No. We're not politicians. But we want to know if you are acquainted with Rick Solomon."

"What's it to you?"

Luke regained his courage and held up his wallet. "We're police, and if you don't help us, we will get a warrant to search your property."

Rick's grandmother was talking to herself. "Rick," she said without addressing the name with her eyes. "What has he done this time?"

Carl and Luke exchanged glances. "We can't answer that question right now, ma'am," Carl said. "But we just need to know where he slept last night."

Her tears began to flow freely. "He slept in the room outside."

"Can we have a look?" Luke asked ever so sweetly now.

"I don't have a key," she said, moving into the house and leaving the door open for the two men to follow. Luke still had his hand on his weapon.

Minutes later, Carl held a crowbar in his hands. "We're going in."

Rick's door was as impregnable as a fort.

"Whoa, whoa, whoa!" retorted Luke. "Don't you think that we need some kind of green light from Captain Cole before we break in there like this?"

Carl didn't have time to get permission from anyone. Every passing minute was too critical. "You didn't see what he did to Carol, did you? I'm not waiting."

Luke replied, "Don't we still have to follow rules and regulations?"

Carl looked at him. "Let me tell you something. If I need any R & R, I'll go to Hawaii. Until then, help me get the goddamned door open, will you?"

Luke kicked the door open. Carl still held the crowbar. He said, "That's the attitude."

The two detectives entered the room. Carl found the light switch and looked about. Luke trailed in reluctantly, hanging back as much as he could. A certain quaintness caught them off guard. Carl expected it to be a crap hole, an abattoir, but Rick's room was spotless and undisturbed. Everything was clean. He left no clothes tossed on the chair. His bed was neatly made, as if it hadn't been slept in. It was evident that Rick was the type who loathed coming home to mess and clutter.

"Nice boobs!" interjected Luke, staring at a 1986 *Playboy* calendar in one corner. The calendar featured a sexy nude blonde with big nipples.

Carl agreed. "Very nice." He moved to the window, looked out at the lowering fall sky, and then at the neighboring duplexes across the street.

"Look at that ass," drawled Luke, staring at the blonde with lustful eyes. "Isn't that a shame she's got to sit on it?"

Carl was annoyed, "You notice anything else?"

"No."

"He has the room furnished like a jail cell. Nothing more, nothing less."

Luke put his gloves on and said, "Well, at least he's neat and clean."

While Luke wrenched open the fridge, Carl skirted around the room overturning the chair, mattress, and everything else there was to turn. Then he stepped into the tiny bathroom. It was just as clean as the main room, and it smelled of a lemon-scented air freshener. And no water was dripping from the shower faucet.

Turning to Luke, he said, "There has to be something here."

Luke pulled an old pillow out of a trashcan and inspected its contents. He held up a newspaper clipping. "Look at this!"

"What is it?"

"A clipping from Connecticut about an attorney who was killed in a boating accident."

"And?"

"It doesn't give any details. The police are still investigating."

Carl carefully took the clipping from Luke, scanned it, and then walked back over to the trashcan while Luke made another discovery. "Well, he can't be too dumb. He knows how to spell his name."

Deep in thought, Carl turned to Luke and asked, "What? What'd you say?"

"Look," Luke said, pointing at the letters on the ceiling.

"*K … C … I … R.* Yeah, I guess he's smarter than you, because he can write his name backwards."

Luke said, "Maybe he's one of those people who has dyslexia."

Carl nodded. "Maybe it means something. It must mean something."

"Maybe it's his line."

Carl asked, "Line? What kind of a line?"

"Poetry line, maybe."

Carl shook his head, clearly disgusted with himself. "Nonsense."

"And maybe he's playing with us as he watches us from the shadows."

A tremor passed through Carl as he looked out the window at the shadows on the street.

"You're right. He's playing with us. The exact same way he played with Carol."

"Know what?" continued Carl, his voice confident. "This is a lead. If he took the time to carve three of these letters into the damn ceiling, they must be important to him."

Luke agreed. "True. But let's get the hell out. This place is giving me the creeps."

Carl nodded, not looking at Luke. He was still studying the letters in the ceiling, trying to imagine what Rick was thinking when he put them there. He tried to imagine what the letters meant. Why had Rick carved three letters and had drawn the fourth one with a black magic marker? Beyond any hope of rational explanation, he *knew* this was more than a lead.

Luke tapped him on the shoulder hard enough to get his attention. "We'll come back for him."

With considerable effort, Carl forced himself to focus on Luke and said, "He's not coming back."

And they left.

Back at the police station, Luke analyzed the newspaper clipping as Carl played with the four letters on a tablet. He was having another bad day, physically, emotionally, in every way, and it was only 7:00 pm. Hunched over his desk, he reviewed his notes again. He sensed some specific underlying organization to the puzzle. Something he wasn't getting, some connection he wasn't making. Something awful. Terrible. He could just feel it in his gut.

"Why backwards?" he said. "Why take time to cut three letters into the ceiling, and then write the fourth one in with a magic marker?"

He started pronouncing the letters one at a time. "K, K ... C, C ... I ... R ..."

He said, "C, I, C, I, C ... Carol. I ... Isabelle." Carl froze. A grin appeared on his face as he yelled, "I got it! I got it!"

Luke said, "Got what?"

"The C is Carol, the I is Isabelle, R is Rachel. Who was the fourth woman on the cruise?"

"It was Kathy. Kathy with a K."

*RICK.*

Carl laughed. "He just gave us his agenda."

"But the transcripts showed that Kathy moved to Idaho and that she didn't testify."

"You think a serial killer has a problem driving across state lines?"

Luke nodded in agreement. Carl said, "Get Idaho on the line. Tell them she needs some protection."

Luke left. Then Carl froze as he came to the stunning realization that the K did not stand for Kathy. It stood for Kim. Suddenly, Carl felt a dull ache in the pit of his stomach. He went over his notes again, but there was no mistake. Not by him. The transcripts were accurate. Kathy was on the cruise, but she didn't take the stand during the trial. So the message was perfectly clear. Initially, Rick set out to get even with Carol, Isabelle, and Rachel. Then when Kim stole from him, he included her name on his execution list.

*RICK.*

A feeling of tranquility descended upon him as he reminded himself that Kim was safe on the ship with her dad and that Rick wouldn't find her. But when City Bank called shortly after to confirm Rick's credit card was used to buy a ticket on the M.S. *Redemption*, Carl was a lot less tranquil. He felt mentally and physically drained.

"What's the matter?" Luke asked, seeing the confused look on his face.

"City Bank called. Rick's credit card was used to buy a ticket on the M/S *Redemption*."

"That's good. We'll have Ross grab him."

"No. That's bad," Carl said. He felt cold. Chilled to the bone. He could feel the tremors down his legs and the prickling of sweat over half his body. Every negative emotion hit him at once. He wasn't sure he could do much, but he understood what he was up against and would do his best.

# CHAPTER 13

ROSS AND KIM ENTERED the Victory Dining Room as the sun was setting and the ocean was turning gold in the fading light. Kim flashed a picture as Ross sat down at a table with two other couples, Trevor Davenport and his wife, Paige, and John Ash with his companion, Dolly Sims.

"Hello. I'm Trevor Davenport," Trevor said, effecting the introductions. "This is my wife, Paige." Then he pointed to John and Dolly. "This is John and his friend Dolly."

Ross saw John move closer to Dolly, indicating she was taken. John was a chubby redhead who weighed at least two hundred fifty pounds, most of it in his belly. Dolly wasn't any of that. Quite the opposite. Tall. Statuesque. Totally stacked. A short-haired brunette, marked by experience. Strangely, this woman had September's blue eyes, high cheekbones, white teeth, widely spaced breasts, supple body, and a sweet and sparkling smile. Incredible. She was wearing a clinging pink sweater and a tight white skirt that accentuated her waistline and her bottom. Dolly was so strikingly attractive that for a brief moment Ross entertained the thought of touching the corner of her luscious pink lips, experiencing the warm, fluttering-tingling-melting of sexual desire.

Ross said, "And I'm Ross Leblanc, and the flighty one who doesn't know where she's sitting is my daughter, Kim."

Right on cue, Kim approached and said, "And I'm the official Leblanc family photographer, or no one would know that we were ever alive." Kim pushed on Ross as their assigned waiter, Julio, walked up.

If Elvis had undergone cosmetic surgery to improve his appearance, he might have been as handsome as Julio. Short dark hair, blue eyes, dimpled chin, soft spoken, he had a gentle quality to his good looks that could drive women crazy. "I'm Julio, your waiter. Would you like a few minutes before I take your order?"

"No," John retorted sharply. "I know what I want. I just want fish. Lots of fish."

Ross looked at John and wondered if anyone had ever taught him any manners. Julio said, "Any preferences?"

"Give me the orange roughy."

Julio said, "Excellent selection, sir."

Then John changed his mind. "I want snapper. That's what I want."

Julio turned to Dolly. His attention was now divided between her eyes and her sweater, which revealed too much of her breasts. "What about you, ma'am? I meant to ask you first. Anything *special* for you?" Excitement filled his voice.

John cut in, "She'll take fish, too. Thank you, and get me another drink."

Julio signaled for a busboy. Then, to make matters worse, as the busboy caught sight of Dolly's breasts, he accidentally spilled a pitcher of water on John's lap. That made John incredibly furious. "Get away from me, damn you!" John snapped.

The busboy backed off, tripping and nearly breaking his leg against another table. And then Ross understood the implications of John's behavior. He was jealous. Terribly jealous.

Dolly smiled back sexily at Julio. A smile, to Ross, where plenty was said, and yet no words were spoken. "Please call me Dolly, sweetheart. And, no, I don't want fish," she said, scowling at John. But her eyes seemed to be sending out secret loud and clear messages that Julio longed to decipher. "So, allow me a moment to scan the menu once more."

Ross turned his attention away from Dolly to Kim. "Tell me when dinner's over. I can't take much more of this table, or even her."

Dolly overheard Ross's remark. Kim elbowed him to shut up.

"Very nice meeting you, Dolly. Please take all the time you need. I will be your assigned waiter for the voyage," Julio said, returning his face quickly to the aggravated John. "Soup or salad, sir?"

"Salad."

"We have all kinds, sir. Anything in particular?"

"Whatever. Just bring me some salad."

Calm as a clam, Julio said, "Whatever you say, sir. Dressing?"

Dolly was clearly annoyed by John's sour mood. Ross could tell where this was heading.

"Jesus Christ! Whatever," John said irritably. "Just bring me some goddamned salad."

Kim was laughing. Trevor and Paige were shaking their heads with embarrassment. Ross and Dolly had been trying not to stare at each other all night. But now neither one looked away. Evidently Julio wasn't intimidated by John's pathetic behavior. He remained under control and very cool under pressure.

"We have Thousand Island, blue cheese, Italian, low-cal French, Sweet 'n' tangy, Parmesan pepper … Sorry."

"You've got peanut butter?" asked John.

"That's a negative, sir," Julio replied regretfully. "We do not have peanut butter on board the vessel, sir."

"What kind of freaking dining room is this?" screamed John, clenching his fists, as if he was on the brink of hitting Julio in the face. His actions suddenly drew the attention of almost the entire dining room.

This was Ross's bad luck.

"And your fish, sir," continued Julio, ignoring his sarcasm. "How would you like it cooked?"

"I want it broiled with onion. Lots of onion. Do you understand that?" he lashed out with sarcasm.

Julio shook his head. "And what would you like to eat with the fish, sir?"

"Potatoes."

"Potatoes?"

"Yes. *P-o-t-a-t-o-e-s*." he said slowly, spelling it out. "Do you understand the English language?" Laughter filled the entire dining room. People from several tables away were sparkling. Kim was laughing so hard tears were actually streaming down her cheek.

Ross wondered if crew members were supposed to be nice to this extent. If he were Julio, he'd probably have kicked John's ass.

"Would you like butter, sour cream, cottage cheese, cream cheese? We've got lots, sir. You name it, we've got it."

More laughter.

"No butter! No cheese," shrieked John. "No nothing. Is that clear?"

Julio said, "Like the crystal clear water, sir. And how about vegetables?"

Shrill, riotous laughter erupted from everywhere in the dining room. "Just kidding," said Julio.

That was it. John rose from the table. "I'm getting enough of this shit. Who's in charge in here?" Just then the maitre d' appeared and sat him back down and dismissed Julio from the table. He informed John that Julio was a born comedian, and that was the way he worked. "However," he added, "I could assign you another waiter if you wish."

John said nothing. He was satisfied or repulsed. Hard to tell which.

"So what would you prefer?" demanded the maitre d'. Everyone was laughing. Ross couldn't help it and joined in with the others. Trevor was cackling like a hen. Dolly's face turned pink with laughter. Kim excused herself from the table. Paige followed suit. Then the maitre d' started laughing hysterically along with the other guests.

As for John, he gave the maitre d' a glance, and that was enough to make him back off without saying another word.


Derek took two seasick pills and lay down. "Go on out. I'll be all right."

Rachel kissed him. She was the perfect girl. She told Derek that she was the type of girl he could depend on as much as she could depend on him. In good times and bad times. "I'll get a sandwich and watch the tube. Those seasick pills are going to knock you out."

Shortly thereafter, Derek passed out. Lying on her back next to Derek, head on a pillow, heart in peace with no twinge of remorse, Rachel suddenly thought about her deceased parents. May Richards, her mother, was a gem. She was a sweet and honest woman, faithful, undemanding, and easy to please. Her father, Bruce Tolar, was a life coach. He would always say, "You can have anything you want if you believe in yourself. Always do the right thing. Live a good, honorable life. Then when you get older and think back, you'll enjoy it a second time." When Rachel turned sixteen, her dad used to give her advice as she was preparing to go out on a date. She was filled with all the energy and enthusiasm of extreme youth. Bruce had instilled in his only child a firm sense of confidence and self-worth.

"Turn. Let me see you," he would say approvingly. "You're so stunning, princess." Then he would add the words he always said before she went out, words every daughter needs a father to say: "Now remember, before you go into the dance, pause a moment at the doorway, lift your head, and tell yourself, 'I am the most beautiful girl at the ball.' And only *then* go in." He was teaching her confidence, infusing her with aspiration and vitality. It was a great feeling knowing that her folks had always believed in her. But now it dawned on her that she dreadfully missed her parents and that she had also lost their greater gift.

Derek turned on his back. As she stared at him, she recalled the good-looking masseur from Wales she had met in the spa on her very first cruise. He'd made her explode in a burst of moans and shouts. The memories of her encounter in the massage room were still vivid in her mind: The masseur led her into his room, locked her inside, and took a hike, which was a part of his procedure. Then she completely stripped and lay face down on the couch as instructed, and waited. He went to work the minute he reappeared, putting on his professional smile, his talented fingers relaxing her body. She was already wet and ready to come. When he instructed her to turn over, she thought it was about time. He attacked her with his tongue, exploring her teeth, her gums, licking the roof of her mouth. Then his tongue slid into her ear. She breathed deeply. Unable to resist, she got up, unbuttoning his shirt, dragging it from his wide shoulders, and going for his fly.

Dismissing the thoughts, she scanned the ship's newspaper and learned that this week's voyage marked the ship's first full year of service as the world's largest cruise liner. Over the course of the past year, the M/S *Redemption* had covered thirty-eight thousand nautical miles and had carried two hundred eighty-five thousand people on Caribbean cruise vacations, achieving an average occupancy level of 111.1 percent. During that time, the ship held the record for the most passengers carried on a single voyage—3,633. The crew had served 175,650 pounds of prime rib, 101,980 bottles of champagne, 274,000 bottles of wine, 45,000 pounds of salmon, 1.4 million shrimps, and 321,000 pounds of chicken.

Additionally, passengers and crew members had utilized 6 million bars of soap, 6.7 million rolls of toilet paper, 42,000 towels, and 60,000 light bulbs. In the Nautica Spa, where Rachel had already booked a full-body massage, the staff had provided 18,901 massages, 5,378 slimming treatments, 8,208 facials, and 1,723 personal fitness consultations. Based year-round in Miami, the M/S *Redemption* sailed twice a week to the Bahamas.

When the bellboy arrived with Rachel's turkey sandwich, she flicked on the TV. To her surprise, *Cape Fear* was on. The remote control trembled in her hand. Frustrated, she bit her tongue almost hard enough to draw blood. A quiver passed through her, leaving her shaking uncontrollably.

Rick Solomon stepped out of the Jubilation Dining Room holding a can of Coke, a toothpick clenched between his front teeth. Black shades concealed eyes of death. He looked down at the dwindling crowd on the Empress Deck in front of the purser's office, removed his glasses, and saw Kim with an older man. The long blonde hair. The wholesomely pretty face. The height. The walk. And the knockout body. "I can't be this lucky," Rick whispered to himself.

Call it luck, fate, or whatever, but Rick couldn't believe she was the very same blonde girl who had made the drop on Friday. He watched her kiss the man's cheek and stroll under the Grand Atrium toward the bank of elevators. Rick rocketed after her and made it just in time to get to the elevator before the door was closed. "Hold that elevator, please."

Kim said, "Floor?"

"Lido. Thanks." Rick surveyed Kim, his eyes cold. "Having a good night?" he asked her.

"Can't complain. You?"

And just before Rick could think of anything to say, Kim said, "Cool sunglasses!"

He used his charm. "You can try them on."

Rick handed her the sunglasses. She put them on. Her fingers were long and perfectly formed, the nails painted chocolate brown.

"They're great," Kim said.

Jazz was piped into the elevator from overhead speakers. Rick winked at her reflection in the glass elevator and moved closer to Kim. "You know you remind me of someone."

Kim laughed as she gave Rick back his sunglasses. "Who? The last girl you laid?"

Rick said, "Uh! Feisty."

Then a strange look came across Kim's face as she stared at Rick. "That's strange. You remind me of someone, too, but he's dead."

"I guess people die every day."

The cabin decks above the elevator door began to light up one after the other: Empress, Sports, Atlantic, and then stopped. Then the moment of truth. "So, what's your name?" asked Rick.

She gave Rick a false name as she extended her slender right hand for him to shake. "Sam Leblanc."

The elevator doors opened with a soft hum. Rick also lied. He stared at her gracious neck and curbed wild impulse to reach out and squeeze the life out of her. "Jim Cuomo," he said. "Pleased to meet you, Sam. So, what is there for young people like us to do on this ship?"

Kim said, "Whatever you can get away with."

Rick's smile broadened, and some of the hostility went out of it. "And you?"

"I'll be dancing my feet off later, if you want to find me."

Kim smiled as she exited the elevator. Rick watched her go. She looked great. Good enough to eat. He had to admit it. She was *meant* to be stared at, and he didn't have to conceal this truth from himself.

Rick waved. *You bet your ass, bitch.* "Me, too," he said.

Carl felt ill and inadequate. The air in the room seemed suddenly moist and oppressive. The realization that Kim, Rachel, and possibly Ross might be dead soon struck him as particularly eerie.

Luke was unsuccessful calling the M/S *Redemption*. "It's still busy."

Carl grabbed a telephone and called Cole's house. The phone was picked up on the second ring.

"Hello?"

"Captain Cole, please."

"Is that you, Carl?" asked Pamela. She was the same age as Cole, a very attractive woman despite the extra twenty-five pounds she carried.

Carl lowered his hands from his face. "Yes, Aunt Pam."

"Something wrong?"

"No. No. I'm all right, Aunt Pam—"

"You sound upset," she said, interrupting him. "Are you sure?" Her voice was low, almost a whisper.

Carl was in such furious distress, he said, "No, I'm fine. Please put Uncle Cole on. It's an emergency."

Pamela was silent. Then she said, "Hang on a sec. I'll get him."

Cole came on the line a second later and said, "Carl, what's happened?"

"We need you here. Kim's in trouble."

"Kim who?"

"Ross's daughter. And worse, I just found out that the killer is aboard the M/S *Redemption* with them."

"Hold on. You're telling me that the killer is aboard the same ship with Ross and Kim? How can that be?"

Carl's throat was dry, and he licked his lips.

"He's after Rachel."

"Who's Rachel?"

Carl hesitated just a fraction before answering. "Our witness."

"What's our witness doing on a boat?"

"I'll have to explain that."

"You're right. You will."

Cole hung up.


Captain Cole sat at his desk staring blankly at Carl as though he had spoken in a foreign language, a language that Cole didn't understand. "You know," Cole said, "ten years ago, I would have said, 'Not a chance.' But these kids today … damned if I know."

"Wonder if Rachel has any remorse," said Luke.

Cole shot back, "Probably none. Forgetfulness is the core of the mind. I've seen too much of people's fiendish brutality. Just last week another Rachel from South Carolina drowned her own two children and blamed it on a black guy." He shook his head with disgust. "Any luck contacting Ross?"

Luke said jokingly, "The only operators that speak English are cruising on another ship."

Captain Cole was furious. "Give me the telephone."

Cole took the phone and got an operator. "You American?"

The operator said, "Yes, sir."

"Then speak to my man here. It's an emergency." He handed the phone back to Luke. "You lose him, you'll be playing meter maid for a week."

Cole motioned for Carl to follow him in the hall. He looked both ways and said, "You actually left a package of heroin in the hands of a seventeen-year-old girl?"

Carl suddenly looked older and ill. His eyes were wide with concern. "She was in danger."

"I guess we're all capable of making bad decisions." He paused. "But didn't you also say a senior detective took possession of the heroin that's being safeguarded in his safe-deposit box?"

Carl caught on. "Yes, yes." he said, trying with all his might to maintain self-control.

"And now off the record, nephew," said Cole quietly. "Ross didn't know anything about this, did he?"

To Cole's relief, Carl said, "No. And he still doesn't know anything's happening."

Cole glanced at his watch and sighed with annoyance. "A big, modern ship like this with satellite trouble! Isn't that ridiculous?"

Carl nodded in agreement. Cole stroked his beard and said, "What's the exact location of the ship?"

Carl said, "Somewhere between Miami and Freeport."

"Look," lamented Cole. "I'm going to check with the DA to see what I can get away with legally without blowing the case. Stay put."

Within an hour, Carl and Luke stood in the briefing room with seven other special agents as Captain Cole moved to the lectern.

"Okay, people," began Cole, "We seem to have a satellite problem with the ship, plus long distance operators that don't speak English."

He removed his wire-frame glasses, placed them on the lectern, and said, pitching his voice low enough to avoid being threatening while still maintaining authority, "You are leaving as soon as possible. If the cruise ship makes it to Freeport in the Bahamas, the next stop, it's too late. We have a killer aboard with three potential victims. One is Ross, an officer with this department. Any questions?"

Detective Freddie Jones raised his hand and said, "Captain Cole, do we know for sure that Solomon is on the ship?"

An irritated look spread across Cole's face. "Yes, Freddie. He *is* on the ship. For sure."

"Another thing," added Freddie. "Instead of flying us over to meet the ship at sea, why can't they just turn the ship around? There has to be other options."

"I've outlined them already."

An FBI agent spoke up. "This Ross. Can he help us?"

"If the satellite comes back on, maybe. But the problem is, he'd have to look through three thousand people, and he has never seen Solomon."

"An unconfirmed report states that the suspect is armed to the teeth," said another detective with blond hair, a pug nose, and a square face. "Is that correct?"

"We can't confirm that at the moment. But I know that all passengers must pass through a metal detector before boarding the ship. This meeting is adjourned."

# CHAPTER 14

KIM CHANGED INTO A pair of Duck Head shorts and an oversized navy blue lace-up ribbed cotton shirt. She then ducked into the disco, a place not to be missed. It offered a state-of-the-art sound and light system, as well as a sophisticated array of high-tech lasers and pyrotechnics. According to the ship's newspaper, at ten o'clock it was the place to be if you were single.

Kim glanced at her watch. It was 9:57 PM. Perfect timing. The place was already packed. The music was blasting, and good-looking people mixed with ugly ones on the dance floor. Young and old horny cruisers abounded, circling several standing stations, where you could place your drinks and survey the action. Everybody seemed to be on the prowl. The ambiance carried an air of total unreality. Two boys stared at her perky boobs and licked their lips as she strolled past the bar. Kim pretended not to notice.

As she looked about, hoping to see Jim, she spotted Ross sitting on a stool around the dance floor. He was nursing a Miller light. "Dad," she cooed, "I've been looking all over the place for you. Thought you were supposed to wait for me in the piano bar."

Ross said, "I did. And then I gave up and came here, knowing you'd probably be here, too. What took you so long anyway?"

She complained hotly. "I needed to change, remember?"

Ross shot back. "Half an hour to change?"

"Sorry," she said, sliding onto a stool. Ross turned his head as Dolly, Trevor, and Paige made their entrance into the disco. "There they are again."

Kim saw them coming over. Dolly, too, had changed into a dress that oozed over her curves, barely making it across the famous boobs. She was smiling at Ross and Kim. Her step was light and confident. She had the step of a cheerful woman.

"Dad," retorted Kim. "Quit being so mean."

91

The music changed to a horny Bryan Adams singing "Heaven." Trevor waved at Ross as he dragged Paige to the jam-packed dance floor. They started moving their bodies in an exuberance of joy and passion. And to Kim's surprise, Dolly said, "Would you care for a dance, Mr. Antisocial?"

Ross joked, "As long as Johnnie doesn't object."

"He has no right to have any objections."

"Really?"

Dolly said, "He buys a ticket for the same cruise I'm on. He buys the cheapest stateroom on the lowest level of the boat. I think he hoped to be upgraded to my room." She paused and exchanged glances with Kim. "What can I say? If the boat springs a leak, he will be the first to feel the water."

Ross laughed. "Come on, then," he said to Dolly and pulled her out onto the dance floor.

Kim said, "Way to go, Dad! Go on and show her what you've got!"

Kim laughed, feeling greatly relieved. Over the past seven years, it grieved her that Ross seemed inclined to remain single. Sometimes she looked at him and could feel the sense of loss in his eyes, the deep and terrible ache a child feels when he realizes he had gone wrong somewhere. All the landmarks were strange, and he no longer knew how to find his way home. She always wished she could bring him back the happiness he was desperately craving. But now, no matter how long it might last, she saw a spring of hope because he looked happy, full of life. If anything, he looked better than ever. He looked stronger, clearer, and certainly not lonelier than a man could endure. He actually looked rather handsome for an older man.

As Ross and Dolly giggled like kids, Kim figured that the woman could possibly herald the future, a happy life for her, and come to be everything that a man like her father wanted in his life. She was exotic, charming, and funny, and she seemed to be smart and sincere. And, she had Ross under her spell. Their bodies fit together like pieces of a puzzle. She wondered if they would end up in bed later.

Kim was ordering a pina colada, when an unattractive kid who looked like a refugee from Hells Angels approached her. He was tall and skinny, as if he were suffering from a touch of malnutrition. He was wearing more jewelry than Mr. T. His T-shirt was emblazoned with the words "If we are what we eat, I could be you by morning!"

Kim wanted to ignore him as he tried to strike up a conversation. "D-didn't I speak to you in the lounge earlier on tonight?" he said, the desperate eyes and the twitch going full force. Accustomed as she was to men approaching her, she had never quite figured out a way to repel them without getting involved. She hated it. But now she stood her ground, and a petulance crept into her voice. Kim glanced up at the skinny boy. "Nope," she said.

The boy took a swig of his beer. His verdict was definitely thumbs down. "Well," he said, viewing her speculatively, "if that wasn't you, then can we dance or something?"

"I like your shirt. If we are what we eat, I could be you by morning."

The boy smiled and moved closer. He smelled like a cool breeze from a camel's ass.

Kim fixed him with her devastating blue eyes and said, "What have you been eating? Porcupines?"

She started laughing as the boy swiftly moved away. And suddenly, a voice from behind her rang out: "Damn, you're cold." She turned to see Rick smiling at her. Kim smiled back. "Jim, I was only cold because earlier tonight when I walked by that schmuck, he licked his lips as if it were a promise to come."

Ross waved at them. Rick waved back. "Are they your parents?"

Kim said, "No. Only the horny one. He's my dad."

Rick grinned. "He's not going to be horny long."


Ross was getting horny on the dance floor and had raised quite a boner inside his pants. Dolly's gorgeous thighs were giving it healthy twangs with every step they took as they danced to the soulful sound of Tina Turner's hit song "What's Love Got to Do With It." He delighted in the warm softness of her breasts squeezing against his chest. The scent of fragrant hair flung across his face. Definite signs of arousal spurred him on, setting his heart racing. Inner amusement brought an added sparkle to Dolly's eyes to match the pasted-on grin. The feeling was almost magical. Contrary to the way he felt before he boarded the ship, at this very moment he wanted to love, and he wanted to live forever, if possible.

As they moved their bodies fluidly to the last minute of the song, Ross pursued the early topic of conversation. He said, "Thought he was your man."

Dolly gave Ross a look that asked, *Are you crazy?* "Him? No way," Dolly said.

"Could have fooled me by the way he was acting."

Dolly said, "Could you imagine me dating a man like that?"

Ross smiled. "No, I couldn't. I'm sorry."

"Shh," she said, reaching out to touch his lips with her index finger. "No apology is necessary." She smiled. It was sweet and lovely, that smile, perhaps the more so because it wasn't complicated by much in the way of thought. "You just didn't know." She closed her eyes and moved her body in harmony with Ross.

Ross needed an excuse to meet Kim's new friend. So when the song was over, they checked on Kim. "Who's your friend, honey?"

Kim said, "This is Jim. Jim, this is Dad and Dolly."

Rick shook hands with them both. "Nice meeting you."

Ross gazed at Rick. "Haven't I seen you before?"

Rick's attitude became guarded. Ross noticed the change. "I don't think we've met."

Then Ross offered a smile. "Yeah, that's right. You're the Peeping Tom on the top deck."

Rick said, "Never know where I might see birds."

They all laughed.

Ross relaxed. "Anyway," he said to Kim, "me and Dolly are going up on the top deck for some fresh air. You wanna tag along?"

Kim shook her head. "Nah."

"Are you sure?"

Kim smiled. It was a smile that perhaps indicated that a walk upstairs was supposed to be romantic, but only for him and Dolly. "No, Dad," she said, much to his pleasure. "We'll stay here."

"Suit yourself! And I'm sure that Jim here can take care of my seventeen-year-old daughter. Can't you, Jim?" he said, establishing the parameters between the two of them.

Rick answered, "I definitely will take care of her, sir."

Ross didn't hear. The pounding of the speakers was deafening. "Excuse me?"

Rick repeated, "Oh, I said, most definitely, sir."

Ross kissed Kim on the cheek. With Dolly on his arm, he navigated his way through the crowd toward the exit door.

There were exciting times ahead for the both of them on the after section of the Lido Deck.


After meeting Ross and Dolly, Rick and Kim sat in the lounge on the Promenade Deck getting acquainted over a Coke and a Miami Vice. Rick was staring closely at Kim, and she noticed. "Why are you staring at me?" she asked, looking as sweet as ever. Her skin glowed, her hair was a rich yellow gold, and her figure was voluptuous, without one inch of fat.

Rick said, "I thought you were someone else. A deceitful bitch."

Kim frowned. "Uh! Rough talk."

"But she wanted to play games, and that's not you."

Kim raised a cynical eyebrow and made a face. "Good," she said, changing the subject. "So, what do you do?"

He took a pull on his Coke. She did the same to her Miami Vice. "Right now, I'm just settling debts."

"I mean for a living."

"I'm between jobs."

She regarded him through narrowed eyes. "Before that?"

Rick wondered if she suspected something about him. "Before that, I did a little bit of everything, really."

"Like what? Tell me. I'm curious," she said.

"I plan events, mentor kids, do some volunteering."

"That's very admirable." She was flirting with him, pulling out all the stops and getting hot in the process. Her breasts rose, nipples swelling. "Have anyone special in your life?" she asked.

"No. I'm a loner. I don't think anyone could put up with me."

Kim searched his eyes, trying to tell whether he spoke the truth. "Ever been married before?" she asked.

Rick pinched the bridge of his nose. "No."

Kim continued to stare at him as she played with her hair, making little ringlets by her ear. "Been close?"

Rick smiled.

"Touchy subject?"

Rick said, "Not really."

"You know something? A handsome guy like you ..." She trailed off and kept staring at him. "Never mind."

Rick ran his hand across his chin with practiced charm. "Thanks. I'm flattered."

The guitar player dedicated the next song to the first-time cruisers. Kim said, "First time on a boat?"

"You mean ship."

"Yes, ship. Boat, canoe, whatever."

Rick laughed. "No. You?"

Kim took another sip of her Miami Vice. "Yes. And I like it. You?"

Rick shrugged and made a gesture with his hands. "It's a vacation and nothing else. And I can't wait to get the hell off."

Kim looked at him searchingly. "Why, aren't you having a good time?"

Rick glanced at the festivities from across the bar. It was unreal. Drunken passengers were dancing, even on tables. In the casino, gamblers took over the place. They were in and out with cups of coins in one hand and drinks in the other. The place was a madhouse. Constant action. There were about thirty people at the craps table betting on everything. Every pitch.

"It's too disconnected, you know? It's not real," he said with an emphatic wave of his hand. "Before you know it, all that is going to be nothing more than a figment of your imagination."

Rick sipped his Coke. They lapsed into silence. Kim brought her glass up to her mouth, rolling the sip of Miami Vice upon her tongue before swallowing. "Coke! Don't you drink at all?" she asked.

He met her eyes and smiled. "Haven't needed it for a few years."

"How do you get high?"

"Settling debts and searching for the truth."

Kim said, crossing her creamy legs on the couch, "Whatever. Can you do me a favor?"

"Sure. Anything," said Rick readily, with false modesty.

"Uh, no," she said with an amused glint in her eye. "It doesn't matter."

"What doesn't matter? Spit it out."

He had no clue what she wanted, and he hoped it was nothing too personal.

"I was wondering if you would be able to buy me some weed tomorrow, and I'll pay you back whatever you want."

She sipped her Miami Vice once more. "What do you say, stud?" she said after a short pause, her eyes fastened on him. "Oh," she added, trying to put his mind at ease, "they don't check passengers' bags on their way back from the island."

Rick sipped his Coke. "Why wait—"

Before Rick could finish his statement, as if it was so natural to happen, he saw Rachel and possibly her boyfriend, Derek, enter the Astoria Lounge, where the late show was about to begin. Rick blinked in disbelief. He nearly gaped. Kim noticed the sudden distraction.

"What are you looking at?"

Rick's mind quickly returned to Kim. "Just a memory and nothing else."

At first, he was sure it must be his imagination running wild. Not a day had gone by when had he not stopped thinking about Rachel. But as his eyes followed her, he was certain it was *the* Rachel Tolar—in the flesh. Now he needed an excuse to put Kim on hold, so he could pursue Rachel. He quickly considered a possibility. "But I was about to say, why wait for tomorrow when I can score some shit tonight?"

Kim's face lit up. Her eyes gleamed with excitement. A hearty laugh leaped from her throat. "Really? You can do that?"

Rick nodded wisely, barely able to keep the awe out of his voice. "I have years of practice."

Absently, she touched her breasts beneath her shirt. Her hands pressed the fabric, outlining the nipples. "You know something?" she stated seriously, their gazes merging into one persuasive look of yearning and longing. "The minute I looked at you, I could have sworn that you were a player who could get things."

"What are you, psychic?"

"Little bit."

"Great," Rick said. "But here's what I want you to do: I want you to go to your room, and I'll bring the weed to you later."

She was impatient. Typical woman. "When?"

Rick consulted his watch. "In about half an hour."

Kim proposed in a velvet-soft voice. "Maybe I can go with you."

Deep sincerity entered his voice. "And spoil the surprise? It involves a debt. But I promise after that, you'll receive my complete attention tonight."

A flirtatious smile curved at the corner of her lips. "Okay if I time you?"

"Knock yourself out."

Rick watched her saunter away on her sweet young legs, walking away without a backward glance.

Rick's journey was just getting started.

# CHAPTER 15

CARL TRIED HIS LUCK on the ship-to-shore. The phone began to ring.

*Pick up, damn it! Pick up!*

Cole lit up a cigarette and took a long drag. He sighed with impatience. Carl said, "Those are bad for you."

The phone rang four times.

"So are killers with a twisted sense of fair play."

Five times.

*Gee. Where are they?*

A sixth time.

Then someone picked up the phone on the seventh ring, just as Carl was beginning to despair. "Hello? This is the radio room. Chief radio officer Leonardo Blanco speaking," he said in Italian-accented English. "How can I help you?"

"Hello?"

There was a lot of hiss and static on the line.

"Chief?"

"Yeah, who's calling?"

Chief Blanco's voice was barely audible. More static. Carl put the phone on speaker and backed up.

"This is the Miami Shores police. Can you hear me?"

There was a two-second delay before Chief Leonard said, "Yes, I can hear you." Carl said, "This is an emergency." More static. "You need to locate Detective Ross Leblanc ASAP."

Blanco didn't hear squat. "What?"

"It's an emergency. Find Detective Leblanc now."

The static temporarily abated.

Silence.

Cole said, "Did you copy, chief?"

"Yeah, I copy. But you're going to have to call me back in about fifteen because I don't have the ship's manifest."

Carl said, "Look, chief, we can't hang up."

"But I can't put you on hold. My office is flooded with calls," Blanco said. "I'll find him. Call back."

Cole said, "What part of—"

The line went silent as Carl and Cole looked at the phone.

Carl threw both hands in the air. "It's an emergency!"

The next fifteen minutes passed like snails.



On the top deck, Ross and Dolly clutched each other in hilarity as they stood near the railings.

"You know something?" Ross said, beginning to tenderly massage Dolly's back. They were at the very aft end of the ship, which was now inhabited by just the tawdry few. "When I looked into your eyes in the dining room tonight, I swore that you were a sexual magnet that could attract men from the four corners of the world."

Dolly giggled, her body tingling all over. "You really felt that way?"

Ross was totally amused and surprised at the turn of events. "How couldn't I feel that way?"

"I take compliments well," she said seductively.

Ross kissed her. He inhaled the fresh smell of her hair when it tangled in his mouth. Now he was beginning to massage from her nape down. And when Ross's fingertips found an especially sore spot just to the right of the third cervical vertebra, which he worked with lover's tender touch, Dolly began to groan softly, "Nice. Very nice."

"Love that?" he asked, well aware of the fact she did.

Dolly murmured, "Hmm. Think I'm falling in love. You?"

Ross didn't answer. He pretended he didn't hear her. Did that mean *he* was falling in love with her? That was a question that he had never needed to ask himself before.

*Love? It's impossible,* he told himself. *I can't be in love with a woman I only met a couple of hours ago. I hardly know anything about her. No one falls in love overnight.*

Ironically, he *was* falling in love with her, just like in the movies. He was falling in love with her because he was on a cruise ship, a love boat where anything was possible. It was a unique vacation place where you could find the most beautiful, ugliest, ignorant, smartest, dumbest, most racist, self-absorbed, greediest, most generous, laid-back, meanest, nicest, craziest, funniest, and weirdest people from all facets of life—all in the pursuit of having fun. He was falling in love with her because her effect on him was undeniable. Because he was already feeling extremely lightheaded. Because his heart galloped anew as his hands tracked a fiery path up her back. Because he knew that he was giving her pleasure and was going to be rewarded handsomely. Then, the biggest surprise came when Dolly said, "I've got a bottle of champagne down in the room. Would you care for a glass?" she said, tentatively and hopeful. Her voice was low, seductive, little more than a whisper. It set off darts of fire in Ross's veins.

Care for a glass! Was she teasing him?

Catching her vibes, Ross gave her a to-the-point look. "If I'm going to go all the way down to your room for one single glass of champagne, my darling, we might as well stay up here till sunrise."

She turned to him, her eyes gleaming with anticipation. She knew what he meant. "I guess we better get going before the ice melts. Don't you think?"

Ross kissed her again. He looked at her with dawning admiration and thought how much she reminded him of his deceased wife. September might have said exactly the same thing.

Eyes resting on her luscious lips, he brought his hands from her back to cradle her head and intercepted with another soulful kiss. His lips captured hers with passionate force, stealing her breath and setting her heartbeat into a runway gallop. She returned the kiss with wild abandon. Erratic heartbeats played havoc with her breathing. Her pulse had gone crazy. He knew he had her and must take her to bed now. And fast. Ross let go of her face, claimed her hand. The excitement was creeping over his body like a rash. He said, "Now, it's time to go."

In the room, Ross stood before her and kissed her again full on the lips. It was some kiss. Tender. Forceful. Both giving and taking, seeking and demanding. Abruptly, she edged away, threw herself on the bed, rolled onto her tummy, looked back at Ross, and whispered in a weakened voice, "Are you going to join me?"

Smiling, Ross approached Dolly's bed. He felt like a clumsy dolt. He took off his shirt and stepped out of his pants, but he kept his briefs firmly in place, covering the Leblanc jewels. Dolly claimed his hand and dragged him onto the bed. They started to make out slowly and leisurely, like two athletes at play. She had a marvelous body, sleek and feline, with narrow shoulders, small hips, fabulous breasts, and beautiful legs. Skillfully, he sought out the pressure points that really turned her on, massaging her neck, her shoulders, and slowly, slowly, he started down to her side, her waist, her butt. He skipped the inside of her ass and landed on her legs, and then the back of her knees, her calves, her ankles, and her feet.

"Turn over, please," he instructed, his pulse jumping erratically.

He heard her say, "It's about time, handsome!"

Ross grinned. He pulled down her G-string with his teeth and buried his head between her legs. The close-up clean aroma of her body floated to his nostrils, triggering a memory too elusive, too removed to identify. And when the tip of his tongue journeyed into her privates, Dolly shook as if a torrent of flames tore deep inside. "Nice," she murmured softly. "Very, very nice."

Ross changed positions, allowing her access to enclose his hardness in her hands and bringing her lips down to caress him with her tongue. He wanted to come in her mouth. He felt passion building such as he hadn't dreamed of in years. Luxuriously, they approached their climaxes. Almost breathless, Ross said, "I thought, uh, we were supposed to have a drink."

"I said in my room, but I didn't say what time. You want to stop and have a drink?"

Ross caught his breath. "No," he said thinly.

A different look appeared on her face. "What's the matter?"

Ross heard himself say, "That I loved September and after all the years of grieving, it suddenly stopped and I feel good."

Dolly said, "You're not mistaking an orgasm for this feeling, are you?"

Ross dove back on Dolly and said, "Well, if it is, I want more."

But as soon as he was about to go for the gold, a female voice was heard over the ship's intercom, bringing him to a halt. "May I have your attention, please? Guest Ross Leblanc, from cabin U7, would you kindly contact the information desk immediately? Thank you."

Ross practically froze on top of Dolly. "Did you hear that? They're calling for me."

Dolly was dejected. "Cheese and crackers."

Ross held out a warning hand. "Hey, the second time will be better, if I know my daughter is all right."

She knew he was right. Ross dressed and silenced her with another soulful kiss. "I'll be back faster than you can spit sideways."

She murmured with sultry eyes, "You promise?"

Ross said, "On my daughter's life."

And he was gone.


In the Astoria Lounge, where the Midnight Special commanded a full and faithful audience partly because it was rated R, Rick Solomon impatiently watched Rachel and Derek. His heart rolled in a storm of rage. What he had inside for her was not just anger. It was a lot more. For three years, he had lived with a burning hatred of her. He wanted her like a sword searching out an opponent with an immediacy that was unusual even in him. Seeing her now, he could hardly wait to hammer her face, split her lips, drive her to her knees, jerk her around, bend her double, kick her like a football, make her beg for mercy, hammer a nail through her heart, and then set her on fire.

After the show, Rick followed them a short distance back. They strolled along the Promenade Deck and ducked into the casino. Impatience plagued him as never before. In the casino, the whizzing and rattling of the slot machines was intermittent. Overhead cameras covered every inch in the room. There were signs and displays on just about every square inch of the walls. Rick watched them exit the casino and cruise along the Promenade Deck, and Rick fell into step behind them. The clock on the wall put the time at twelve thirty-four.

From the Promenade Deck, Rick watched them step into the glass elevator and exit on Verandah Deck. Rick ran up the stairs closely behind them, eager for the hunt to begin. And by the time he made it to the Verandah Deck, he could see them walking down the hall. Rick timed his approach perfectly. No one was lurking in the shadows. Standing around the corner, Rick noticed Derek fish for his key, and they entered the last cabin down the hall. " Good deal," Rick said. "You two are about to have a visitor."

Rick turned and froze.

Kim was coming toward him. She said, "What are you doing here?"

He couldn't believe it. "It's irrelevant. I thought you were waiting for me in your cabin." He watched Rachel's door as it closed.

"I know that." Kim's eyes were full of troubled concern. "But I'm looking for my dad."

"What for?"

"The purser's office called and said that it's an emergency."

"Look," Rick stressed gently, holding her hands in an attempt to calm her down as he put on his most sincere face. "It can wait till morning."

Her eyes fluttered. "Oh, my God," said Kim, looking at his hands.

"What's wrong?"

"Your hands."

Rick could not see what was wrong with his hands, but he asked the question anyway. "What about my hands?"

She grimaced. "They're freezing."

Rick smiled. "Meaning I have warm heart."

Kim shrugged. "I guess," she said hopefully.

For a second, she seemed to be in deep thought, and then she said, edging so close to him that he could feel her breath, "Okay, you're right." And before she started flirting with him again, he said, "Now, go back to the room. When I finish what I have to do, I promise you will be next."

102

Kim pulled a disappointed face. "Next! You make me sound like an agenda."

"Just depends on your point of view. Are we cool?"

By now they were nose-to-nose. Her lips nearly brushed against his. She had an apple body fragrance.

Kim's nod was one of resignation. "I'll be waiting."

Rick reached out, held her face in his hands, and stared at her passionately, their eyes directly aligned to each other. Yet, he was not going to kiss her. He dropped his voice to a musical tone, "I'll be back for you shortly." And he walked away.

Disappearing down the hall, Rick took the nearest elevator. He stopped by the purser's office to borrow a black magic marker. Then he stormed into his room. He wasn't surprised to notice that the room steward had arranged his T-shirt in the shape of an animal.

Placing the mini briefcase on the bed, he extracted a knife, a length of rope, and the .32-caliber pistol. He made absolutely sure that all the rounds were in the chamber, and then he spun the sound suppresser onto the muzzle of the pistol. He needed to be as conservative as possible because the pawnshop guy who had sold him the piece stated that sound might escape after the first six rounds were fired. Satisfied, Rick reached for his life jacket. In the center, he scribbled the words Cruise Staff, and then he was out of there.

Something exceptional was about to happen on the Verandah Deck.

# CHAPTER 16

IT SEEMED TO RACHEL that it had been only a split second ago that consciousness slipped away, and now she was suddenly being jolted awake by a rattling on the door. She had gone to bed feeling positive that something awful was going to happen, something that would change the planned course of this early morning as completely as a cataclysmic earthquake could change the course of a river. Now, half dazed, she watched Derek get up and make his way to the door. He looked through the fish-eye lens in the peephole, turned to her, and said, "It is a staff member wearing a life jacket, sweetheart. I think it's an emergency."

Rachel swung her legs off the bed as Derek opened the door. She saw a pistol appearing through the doorway first. The weapon was silently fired, and Derek fell backward onto the sofa. He was dead in seconds. Rachel froze as a man entered. She felt like a spectator at some unreal scene. Fear gripped her. Her vision blurred. Suddenly she felt weak, as helpless as a baby in a crib. She wanted to yell. She wanted to at least try to alarm her next-door neighbors. But her lips were trembling, her throat clogged, and she couldn't produce the softest sound. The man said, "Don't even think about it."

For a second, she closed her eyes, convinced that she was dreaming. She thought, *He's not real. It's all in my imagination.* But when she reopened her eyes again, the man was still there pointing his gun at her.

"If you raise your voice," the man threatened, "I will empty all the rounds in your skull. Is that clear?"

She nodded and glanced at Derek's body. Her head was splitting. A heaviness crept up and down her legs and arms.

*He's not real. It's all in my imagination. Hallucination caused by stress.*

"Who are you?" said Rachel, her suspicions and fear mounting by the second. Her mind was already like an airborne kite, dipping and diving but finding no resting place. "What do you want?"

The man shot back, "The justice maker of the high seas, or *The Gentleman* if you prefer." He laughed. "Does that satisfy your curiosity?"

There was a frozen instant of pure panic as she realized who the man was. She *wanted* to scream but couldn't. Chest-tightening fear had stricken her numb.

She said, "Oh no!"

Rick said, "Shit, yeah."

Rick Solomon. She was sure of it. Even in spite of the years that had passed. Even in spite of the alteration of his appearance, she knew who he was. She wanted to bolt out of the bed and run, but she was so rigid with fear she couldn't move.

When she had testified against him in court, he had fixed her with the same chilling eyes and hadn't glanced away for even the briefest moment. She could read the same message in his stare: *You're going to pay for it, bitch!*

But that had been three years ago, and Rick was supposed to be behind bars for many years. In the meantime, she had taken precautions to be sure he would not find her when he got out of prison. She had long stopped looking over her shoulder. And now there he was. Yet she was convinced that when she awoke, her headache would be gone, her vision would be clear, and Rick would not be standing in front of her with a gun because it was all in her imagination.

"You're a tough bitch to get a hold of, uh?" Rick removed the life preserver and approached the bed.

*He's not real. It's all in my imagination.*

She could not respond to him. There was an icy lump in her throat that she could not spit out or swallow.

*You can't do anything to me, Rick, because it's all in my imagination. It's all in my mind. Damn it!*

"Why me, you stinking whore?" Rick said.

Rachel was trembling from head to toe. A wild alertness crept into her eyes. She stared at him shocked, in disbelief, willing him to vanish, praying to God that he was nothing more than a specter, a figment of her imagination. But he refused to vanish; he remained—undeviating, real.

*You're not real, Rick. It's all in my imagination. You can't hurt me.*

"You tell me truth, and I won't have to gut you like your other friends," added Rick. "You hear me?"

*Jesus! Did he say other friends?* She managed to say, "Carol?"

Rick confirmed her assumption. "Isabelle, too."

"No." An outright horror was in her voice.

"And they were loyal friends. Too bad they're going to miss the wedding. Carol literally spoke with a forked tongue the last time I saw her. Isabelle said she'd give me anything to let her go. I didn't need anything. So I took her life. And now you."

Suddenly, feelings overwhelmed Rachel. Her fear amplified. She didn't know if she was crying for her friends or for herself, because it was perfectly clear to her that one by one they were all dying for what they had done. And now she was next. For sure.

Rick briefly pressed the .32-caliber pistol into her neck. His eyes suddenly dropped down to the provocative curve of her breasts, which were clearly visible beneath the little pajama set, a rosebud print with lettuce-edged lace-up crop top. Her boy-leg boxer revealed everything on her triangle. "So, tell me, Rachel. Why did you do it?"

Rachel's teeth chattered. "I-I didn't mean to. My lawyer f-forced me." She nearly choked on the words.

"Lawyer or the piece of shit."

"Yes."

Random thoughts raced through her head. She remembered one of her teachers, Mr. Moody. He used to say, "Kids, always tell the truth. The truth has its own reward. Once you hear the truth, everything else is cheap whisky." These words struck her at some deep level. She felt the truth of them deep in her bones. Her throat clogged with anger. Her determination weakened.

"Now tell me something I can believe."

"I'm for real, Rick."

Rick laughed expansively and said, "You know my name. That's good. It helps. Now try another answer."

"No, Rick, you're totally wrong. I told you! My lawyer forced us to testify."

"Who are you trying to fool?"

"I swear it's true," she said, struggling to keep the tremor out of her voice.

Then Rick wagged an accusing finger at her and snapped. "No, you abandoned me for money."

"No, that's not true."

Rage gnashed at Rick. His bloodshot eyes burned her to the core. "Enough of the lies. Did you ever think about me, living in fear every day for three years, until the day that I snapped and no one bothered me again?"

She said nothing. *It's all in my imagination.*

"You lied to the jury, didn't you?" He was virtually speaking through clenched teeth now.

*Imagination.*

She glared at him, still convinced this encounter was a dream, a nightmare. A terrible nightmare. Because the odds against Rick finding her there were millions to one. Astronomical. No chance. But he was there now, confronting her.

"Members of my family didn't want to believe me. If it weren't for my brother, I would still be in prison. And you know the saddest part of it all? They fuckin' killed him because he was a drug dealer. Damn, I hate the fuckin' system and people like you. You all stink. All of you." His face grew dark with anger as he spoke.

Rick spat in her face. It was done before she'd even known he was going to do it, but, of course, she'd known it might come to that. Or even worse.

"It was because of you that I nearly killed myself." He was talking very fast now, running his words together. "Maybe I should have done it because now I've got no career, basically no family, and a future with a stinking record."

Rachel closed her eyes and shook violently. His voice slashed at her.

*It's all in my imagination.*

Rick's testimony pained Rachel in every cell. A torrent of regrets, frustrations, and guilt tore at her. She sat there disbelieving all that was happening, presuming it all was a nightmare, expecting to awaken any time and find herself in her stateroom with Derek alone, expecting that nothing had happened. She just sat on the bed in front of Rick, listening to him with a vague sense of unreality yet awaiting punishment for all the wrong things she had done in her life. She could only guess: *Rick is going to blow my head off.* But Rick removed his knife and handed her the life jacket. "Now stand up and put it on," he said, pointing to the balcony. "We're going for a short walk. Or you'll die right here."

At these words, Rachel's heart sank. She sweated and sweated, and she felt her pulse shoot up to the hundreds, still believing this was a nightmare. A brutal realization swept over her: *He's going to feed me to the sharks.* She prayed, "Please, Lord, get me out of this nightmare, please." She had never been a religious woman. Only now it seemed quite apt to say her prayers, and she did so with fervor.

Rachel stood up and started begging. "Please, Rick, don't throw me overboard. It was my lawyer's decision to pin the blame on you," she said as she fought a cold stab of panic. "I'm very sorry."

Rick stared at her, his chilling eyes as cold as Siberia. "No, you're not. Quit stalling."

His words chilled her. "Give me a chance, please."

"I'll give you the same chance you gave me and plenty of time to think about it while you walk."

With Rachel in the lead, Rick followed her to the balcony. "P-please,

Rick! Please." Her teeth were chattering. Her fear grew to a sickness. At this point, she simply did not understand why she had decided to pin the blame on Rick, and now she didn't believe she had a chance of getting away with it. "Please. I promise you I can get you anything you need."

"Can you give me my time back?"

Rachel didn't respond. Her head seemed full of static, sputtering noise like a shortwave radio.

"Those three horrific years that I spent behind bars?" Rick repeated. "Can you give them back to me?"

Rachel shook her head.

"Exactly what I thought."

Rachel stared at Rick with teary eyes. She felt she could somehow reach him with the raw power of her emotion from the hurt that ran so deep. But Rick didn't seem to be a human being anymore. He was without a doubt a heartless predator. Or something less than that.

Her heartbeats were choking her. "Anything you want. Even my attorney."

A scowl hardened his face. "Now you sound like Mario. Shut up and get over the railing," commanded Rick. "Let's see how good you swim."

Outside on the balcony, the night was clear, and the vast water was calm. A noble full moon was sinking eastward, and millions of the most brilliant stars were shining overhead. Utterly resigned to her fate, Rachel stared at the flat horizon, clenched her teeth, and found the courage to do what she had been unable to do before. "I won't jump."

"Since when was any of this negotiable?"

Rachel glanced back at Derek's body as Rick slipped out his knife. "Then what?"

Rick laughed at her renewed strength. "You know what's ironic?"

Rachel gave him the I-couldn't-care-less look.

"I was invited to that rape party on the ship that night. But I didn't feel it was right."

Rachel now looked intently back at Rick.

"And it was intended for the four uppity bitches from the Verandah Deck, not just you. But the crew wasn't complaining because it was you they wanted all along. So, they didn't mind taking turns."

Rick laughed. "In fact, the casino had a standing bet on which crew member would score with you, and the prize was split seven ways." Rick was savoring every moment. "And the security guard? He wasn't there to save you. He wanted to be number eight. After all, you had already screwed three men in two days. So, the crew didn't figure it was rape to you. They figured you'd see it as only routine and that you had no problem increasing the number to ten men. So jump, bitch!"

Rachel was terrified as she put the life preserver on.

*Mario*, she thought, *"when I find you, I will have you bound, hands and feet, beat the living crap out of your balls, and bury you six feet under.*

She said, "This was all for a bet?"

Rick said, "And now you're going to feed the fishes. I don't want you to sink too fast."

For a brief second, she thought of trying to snatch the gun or the knife out of Rick's hands. Except she couldn't lift her own hands. They were cold. They felt as if weights were tied to them. She felt the muscles bunching on her arms and legs and back. And her fear took on a familiar edge. Now she could only think of one thing: *I'm going to die.* Despite the hard lump of fear rising in her throat, Rachel screamed, "Help! Someone help me!"

"Shut up!"

No one helped. No one even heard her.

Rick pushed Rachel overboard. As she fell, the ocean looked like a trap, beckoning her with one exit and no way to turn back. She knew she was going to die. The fear had left her by the time she hit the water.


Rick watched Rachel's last moments as she fell into the ocean. Moving quickly but calmly, he grabbed Derek's body and dumped it overboard. There wasn't a soul around. He looked at his watch: 1:27 AM. His timing was perfect. He wanted to be back in his cabin before two o'clock. He figured it would take him less than five minutes to be on the upper deck. And if there were no delays, he could teach Kim a lesson about respect in twenty minutes and still have ten minutes to kill. Suddenly, he thought about Gus. He would have been proud of him if he were alive. Then he thought of his grandmother's reactions when she found out about what he had been up to. She would probably drop dead the minute she heard the news. But it was not going to happen because nobody saw him. And as soon as he was through with Kim, he would toss all the evidence overboard, and he would be back in his cabin as safe as a church mouse.

Walking down the hall, Rick was rocking out. *R-e-s-p-e-c-t!*


Pam Lee, the late shift purser's office officer, was a sylph. With her sparkling smile, she could have made a fortune doing TV commercials. She was a striking beauty with natural long dark hair, full luscious lips, short straight nose, and a round Asian face. She told Ross to go up to the radio room immediately because detective Carl Levy had been trying to get in touch with him over the past forty-five minutes. "He said it's an emergency," Pam added in a clear American accent.

The news came like a punch, leaving Ross unsteady. "And where is the radio room?"

Pam said, "It's on the Verandah Deck aft, sir. He's still on the line. I'll call the radio officer right now to tell him you're on your way."

As Ross turned to leave, he understood this as a commotion ensued. Something odd was happening aboard the ship. It was so intense, he felt he could almost have carved it like clay. Several crew members in white uniforms, most likely the ship's officers, were scampering throughout the ship with walkie-talkies in hand. Additionally, he was beginning to feel the motion of the ship. Looking back at Pam, he said, "I'm just curious. Is the ship moving?"

Pam's voice had barely changed, but a new alertness colored it. She whispered to Ross, "No. Man overboard."

Ross's eyes went wide. "Really?"

"Yeah. Go on," she said. "I was told to send you up there as soon as I got a hold of you."

With commendable self-control, Ross made his way to the radio room. As he entered, the officer on duty turned to him. "Are you Detective Ross Leblanc?"

Ross shook his head. "Yes, that's me."

"Go into that room over there, and pick up the phone," he said, pointing to a booth. "There's a lot of static on the lines. It's a Carl Levy."

Ross stepped into the booth and sat down.

The officer said, "We could lose him. So talk quick."

The officer closed the door in time for Ross to hear someone say, "Call the Bahamian coast guard."

Ross said, "Carl. It's Ross."

Carl didn't hear him. He said, "Say again, Ross."

"It's Ross. Can you hear me?"

"Yes, Ross, I can hear you now. Is Kim with you?"

"No."

The ship suddenly pitched and rolled. Ross could feel his weight rolling slightly from side to side.

More static.

Ross heard him say, "Find her. Now."

Ross did not understand Carl. "Yes, she's fine."

"No. Find her!"

"Why?"

Carl didn't sound like himself. His voice was faint and nervous.

He said, "Rick Solomon, the kill—"

More static.

"The ship—"

Ross pressed the receiver tightly to his ear and said, "I can't understand you. You're breaking up."

"Rachel lied. She knew him."

Confusion gnawed at Ross. "Knew who?"

Then Captain Cole spoke up. "The killer's aboard your ship. He wants to kill Rachel and Kim."

Ross wasn't sure he had heard the last word correctly. "He wants to kill Rachel and who?"

"Kim," repeated Cole with a voice that now shook with urgency. "Just go find her now."

It was amazing how quickly one's life could change. Five minutes ago, he was in the throes of an orgasm, but now he was pleading near tears, undergoing rapid emotional shifts. Unconvinced, he said, "Cole?"

"Time's wasting, Ross," Cole said. "Find her now."

The last time a similar iron-hard fear had seized Ross was last Friday morning when he dreamed of being attacked by a man while entering his house. As a homicide detective, he had been exposed to every sort of horror. Seeing mutilated or scalped bodies resulting from accidents or shootings required tremendous physical and mental strength. For someone whose life was on the edge, he seemed fearless in moments of great danger. But because his job, which he enjoyed, demanded psychological vigilance, he always recovered quickly from the emotional level of any encounter.

But now Ross, who was not easily frightened, who was always ready, always watchful, always brave, was now petrified. And with his daughter's life at stake, someone who was an intricate part of his life, a sole and only daughter who meant so much to him, he wondered if he would be able to make it through the night should something bad happen to Kim. Life without Kim, after losing September in the fire, would be an unendurable journey, a blind passage through loneliness and nothingness. And if he couldn't save Kim, he would kill himself. After all, as a policeman, he was regarded as a potential enemy, a prick, a nuisance, a thug even by some of the people he worked with. For the first time in his sixteen years on the force, Ross hated himself for the life he was living.

In seconds, Ross's flesh transformed into plaster, his bones into steel rods, and his sinews and tendons changed into bundles of wires. His head pounded, as if he was about to have a migraine. His throat tightened. Pressure swelled in his chest. A drop of cold sweat trickled down his back and slithered like a centipede along his spine. His stomach churned, and he thought he was going to throw up. But he fought it and choked it back down. The agony was unbearable. It took him an unnatural effort to get up and walk out of the booth.

He wanted to call the cabin to put his mind at rest, but profound fear crept so spider-quick through him that if he called Kim and she didn't respond, he would never make it to the room. He'd be sucked into a slough of black despondency and probably die there on the spot. He knew that he should remain calm, hoping to Christ that Kim was in the room sleeping. He knew that not knowing was ultimately worse than knowing. Having no other choice, Ross trembled on an emotional high wire and made his way back down to his cabin, praying for Kim's life.

# CHAPTER 17

ALL RICK SOLOMON CRAVED was vengeance. Nothing more and certainly nothing less. Vengeance was his business. Only his. Those who had trespassed against him would be harshly punished. And he would waste thousands of lives or even the whole world if necessary. That was the extreme to which he was driven. He wasn't sorry for Derek. He was with the wrong woman in the wrong place at the wrong time. Besides, everything was born only to die. Disappointment was inevitable in life. And because pain was the common lot, Rick believed that one must always accept pain and live without fear and remorse. Whistling a tune he had just made up, Rick knocked on the door of cabin U7.

A surprised Kim stood in the doorway looking out.

"You don't need that, Jim. I'm a volunteer."

Rick punched her in the face. He stood over her as she sat on the floor. Kim's eyes grew wide. She started to cry in great racking sobs. Her eyelids fluttered, and she stared up at Rick as panic swept through her. She wanted to say, "What a psychotic prick!" But she lacked the courage. She had not expected such a violent reaction from him in her wildest dreams. Back in the lounge, he'd seemed to be such a gentleman, such a good conversationalist, such an honest and trustworthy man with self-assurance in his voice. But now he was tying her up like an animal.

Rick said, "I knew you'd say that, slut. And my name is Rick."

Rick knelt in front of the bed where Kim's arms were tied to the bedrails with towels. Another towel covered her mouth.

He said, "I wasn't sure until you chose the name of my brother's main squeeze. Boy, women sure are deceitful bitches." He was shaking his head with more anger. "I guess it's too easy to lie on a boat."

He pulled a knife from his pocket. "You don't even know what my brother had in mind when he gave you the package, do you?"

A look of new terror coupled with bewilderment appeared on her face.

"You're only a debt to him, but a gift to me from one evil brother to another. And, in your case, I like to play with my toys."

He cut her ankles free and pulled down her shorts. "And if you do anything stupid, I'll put one mark on your body for every dollar you stole from me. Do you hear me?"

Kim nodded. *Yes. That is understood. Yes.*

His eyes roamed over her young firm breasts pointing upward, almost exposed beneath her shirt. They were secured by a high-cut brief with embroidered lace trim. Her long cheerleader legs added more temptations. Fear in Kim mounted by the seconds. She didn't mind having sex with him. After all, she had always had strong sexual drives. She thrilled to the quick flash of sex. She knew it would come to that. What she feared was the potential brutality and what her dad might do.

Rick unbuttoned her shirt. It fell open, revealing her full breasts. Kim squinted and saw him lick his lips. He liked what he saw. Kim's heart was in her mouth. She wanted to scream for help. But even if she could scream and be heard, with the dead bolt on the door, any attempt to come into the room to her rescue would fail.

She watched him in fear as he unbuttoned her shorts and pulled them down. Kim could feel the penetrating heat of his eyes on her body as he rammed the knife across her breasts, down her belly, and across her bristling pubic thatch. Her long blonde hair fanned out around her face. She started to feel weak and dizzy with terror, but she clenched her teeth instead. She knew that she must stay still because any wrong movement might bring her death sooner than it could bring relief. Playfully, he tickled her feet as he removed her Nike Airs. She went rigid at his touch. Kim chose not to favor him with a direct gaze. She focused on the gun laying on the vanity, which seemed light years away, and then she mumbled his name behind the gag.

"What do you want?" Rick said, glowering at her. "Have another confession to make, uh?"

*Say yes*, a voice said. *Go with the flow.*

She nodded. Rick allowed himself a smile. It was a thin smile, false, entirely without humor. "It better be a good one," he said, removing the towel from her mouth. "Or we are going to see what you had for dinner."

Kim nodded. *Good. There's a chance for survival after all*, she thought.

"Now what is it?" he said, as if he found the prospect amusing.

"I fucked up," Kim began to confess, knowing that it was imperative to begin psyching herself up before it was too late. Dread made her voice barely manageable. But she looked strong, fully resigned to her fate. "But no matter what brought you on this boat, I'm sure it's got nothing to do with me."

"Wrong," shot back Rick. "Very, very wrong."

Kim bit her lower lip. Tears were streaming from the corners of her eyes.

"Why should I forgive you? Give me one reason. One reason only," Rick said.

Without awareness or hesitation, Kim said the magical words. "Because you are a gentleman. You're not the type of guy who would hurt a lady."

*The Gentleman* was his middle name. Rick *The Gentleman* Solomon had been the name given to him by his grandmother. Until he worked on cruise ships, there were only two people who would ever call him by that name: Gus, who looked very much like him, and his grandmother, who always believed he was so gentle, so sweet, and so softhearted.

Rick smiled. "Finally someone sounds like my grandmother. And it's *The Gentleman*," he corrected. "Not a gentleman."

Catching his vibes, she played along. "That's what I meant. You are *The Gentleman*."

A glint of expression flickered across Rick's face. "Do you mean any of that?"

Kim saw this as her window of opportunity.

Rick regarded her through narrowed eyes. A sprig of hope led her to wonder if he might change his mind.

"Look," she said. "Let's forget about all this, Rick. Cut my hands loose, and we'll go to your room. My dad's going to be here soon, and he won't be happy."

"You're right. The cop's on his way. Why should your dad be happy? Why's he special? If he comes in, I'll kill you both."

Helplessness and frustration enveloped Kim. Fear beat through her like the frantic wings of a dark bird. "But why?" she said, trembling like a cold, wet dog.

"Because you are a woman, and all women are sluts."

Kim quivered with revulsion. "Well, all men are dogs, but I'm not going to waste you."

"You would if you could."

"Doesn't it matter that your brother liked me?"

Kim recognized a crumbled Hallmark envelope that Rick pulled from his pocket.

Rick laughed. "What a brother. Revenge is so sweet. He fucks the cop's daughter that's making his life hell, and he uses her to deliver the addresses of all my victims."

A shocked look came over Kim's face as someone tried to get into the cabin. Rick froze.

A voice rang out. "Kim, it's me, open up!"

Rick stuffed the towel back into Kim's mouth and moved to the door.


Ross knew Kim was in danger when he tried his key and it didn't work. His heart ached, threatening to jump into his throat. His fear had grown and spread like a mold. Almost in vain, he pressed his left ear to the crack between doorjamb, listening for movement or sound.

There was none.

The hall was silent and pleasantly cool. Nothing out of the ordinary. No sign of struggle. The gray-carpeted floor and beige walls were spotless. Halfway along the upper deck stood a white bench marked in red letters: Life Jackets Inside. He stood there for about a minute or so, listening to the great pounding of his pulse roar in his ears, convinced that Rick was in the room with Kim, holding a gun or a knife to her head. To be absolutely sure that U7 was his cabin, he fished out his boarding pass from his wallet and checked his cabin number. His hands felt cold and numb, and for the longest time, he couldn't see where his cabin number was written on the pass.

By the time he was able to make it out, the boarding pass and the wallet almost fell out of his hands. He managed to clutch them at the last second. "Oh Christ," he said, returning the pass to his wallet, which he jammed into his pocket. Holding his breath, he knocked on the door again and yelled, "Kim, it's me, honey. Open the door!"

Silence.

No one replied.

A sinking sensation mixed by dark expectations overcame him as he waited for the slightest noise to come from beyond the door.

There was none.

He listened to his heart. Not bad yet. Fast but steady, as if he was on his mark to run a marathon, and in control. As a policeman, he was always watchful. Always prepared. Prepared for anything. He kicked the door open with his foot. Rick flew backward, losing his grip on the knife. He tried to take aim with his pistol, but Ross kicked the gun out of Rick's hand.


With a rush of emotion that was startling, an inner voice that came out of nowhere told Kim not to panic: *Don't panic. You're Kim Leblanc. The daughter of one of the best detectives who has ever lived. If you manage to have Rick listen to you, you'll get through this. You will free yourself from the straps and survive. Damn it! You will!*

She was about to discover a new Kim Leblanc inside the old one. Her mind had begun to move swiftly.

*But how? I'm strapped. I've got no choice. You, Kim Leblanc, without a choice? Who are you trying to kid? I would if I weren't strapped. That's bull. Remember Mr. Labuy, your homeroom teacher? Oh, him … that bald pervert. What about him? He said you always have an option. There's always something you can do. You are never without a choice. But I can't move. Turn on your stomach. Then what? Pull your body forward and use your teeth.*

Kim stopped arguing with herself. A plan began to form rapidly in her mind.

Ross saw panic in Kim's eyes as Rick drew his knife and regained his footing. Rick lunged across the bed, no more stoppable than an express train. He knocked Ross backward into the dresser. The mirror shattered, the glass dissolving into tens of thousands of gummy fragments. They crashed to the floor. Ross managed to twist his body to dodge the knife thrusts, charged Rick like a madman, and wrestled the knife from his possession. As they rolled on the floor, Rick hit Ross, spun him 180 degrees, and then jerked his hand upward, knocking the knife out of his hand. Ross's head pounded as if it were being split with an ax. Now he couldn't seem to catch his breath.

Ross descended upon Rick like a starved vulture out of the sky, swinging wild punches at him, scrabbling desperately to get the knife. But Rick managed to pin Ross beneath him and pound his face with another blow. The cabin tilted around them. Everything was shaking, as if an earthquake had struck them. Ross tried to get back on his feet, but Rick knocked him back down on the floor. Ross felt his body wedged against the wall by the weight of the madman. He tried to jerk out of Rick's grasp. It wasn't going to happen. Rick was much stronger. He had the muscles of an inmate who spent most of his time behind bars lifting weights.

Waves of pain made Ross feel older and weaker. He could smell the distinct metallic odor of blood. Color spots swam before his eyes. He couldn't feel his head or his arms. He felt pins and needles all over. *Jesus! Have I broken my neck?* The pain was unbearable and fierce. *This is it. I'm going to die at sea just like September.* He felt death pulling at him. He was not going to see Kim or Dolly again. He was never going to finish what he and Dolly had started earlier. Another broken promise. *Please, Lord, please! Make a miracle! Please, do something! Anything!*

For a moment, Ross thought he was going to black out, but terror and saving Kim's life kept him conscious.

Rick regained the knife and was bringing it down on Ross. Rick raised the knife. A strange, sickening smile spread across his face.

Ross watched the knife come down. And he rolled. Fast!

The knife thudded into the floor. Rick stumbled, nearly fell on his face. Ross quickly turned, fully expecting the knife to cleave his back. He saw Rick coming at him with extreme ferocity. He almost froze in place, but he rolled. Again and again.


Kim turned on her stomach, pulled her body forward, and used her teeth to loosen the towels as her dad and Rick scrambled and fought to get the knife. If she could grab the gun, it would be all over for Rick. But how long would that take? A minute? Two minutes? Could Ross hold out a little longer? The little voice came back. *Stop wasting time, you fool! Hurry up or you'll be sorry!* Precious seconds passed as she struggled to free herself. With persistence and determination, she untied the first knot, and then the second one, and she was free of the knots. Glancing at Ross, Kim saw Rick regain possession of the knife, and she knew she had very little time left to save her father.


Rick's persistence paid off as he prepared to finish Ross with the knife, but suddenly he was knocked off Ross. He heard the click of a weapon being cocked. He looked up at Kim. She was holding his .32-caliber pistol, leveled and ready to fire.

Ross tried to reach his daughter to gain control of the weapon, but she moved away from him and continued to point the gun at Rick.

"I lied," she said to Rick, panting and almost out of breath. "I am a deceitful bitch. And you're a dog."

Rick smiled broadly at everything he accomplished and returned the compliment. "And you're a slut."

Kim pulled the trigger, shooting Rick at point blank range. The impact of the bullet threw him violently backward against the wall, spraying blood everywhere. Rick slumped to the floor. The hand holding the knife shook a little, and then stopped. Gazing at Ross, he said, "When a guy says you must forgive your enemies, if not ..." His voice was barely above a whisper.

Ross was breathing rapidly. He managed to shake four words from himself: "You become the victim."

Rick said, "That's ... not ... what ... I ... was ... born ... to ... be."

Ross nodded. "Too late."

Kim dropped the gun on the floor and crouched beside her father.

By the time the staff captain and the chief of security lumbered into the room, it was all over.

# CHAPTER 18

AFTER PONDERING ON A note Rick left in her Bible, Granny read Psalm 41, verse 2: "The Lord will preserve him, and keep him alive; and he shall be blessed upon the earth: and thou wilt not deliver him unto the will of his enemies."

As she closed the Bible, someone rang the doorbell. It was exactly ten o'clock in the morning. Granny squinted through the glass door and saw the two detectives who had come to question her the day before. And she knew that a terrible change was coming.

"Sorry to disturb you, ma'am," said Carl. "But we must have a word with you. May we come in, please?"

There was flatness to Carl that was unmistakable. He didn't even look like the same person he was the day before. Immediately, she felt a cold sweat. At her request, they sat down on a couch. The two detectives exchanged a quick glance, as if they were trying to determine which one of them should speak first. And after a short pause, Carl cleared his throat and said, "I'm sorry to have to tell you that your grandson was killed last night aboard a cruise ship. He was involved in at least three murders."

Granny's heart sank. A headache began to throb at the base of her skull. She felt sucker punched in the gut. Through chattering teeth, she clutched the Bible to her chest and groaned, "Oooh, God … I failed my poor Rick."

Grandma clutched the seat. Her pulse rate soared. Tears slowly coursed down her cheeks. "H-he was the only one left," she said, sucking breath between phrases. Her chest felt tight. "I adored him … with all my heart. I taught him … to be an example … to live by. H-he was a gentleman with a p-promising life, good as gold, until this wrongful …" She wanted to continue, but she couldn't. The words tightened around her throat, squeezing against the base of her skull, forcing more tears to flow.

Carl rose and sat next to her. He offered her his handkerchief and placed a friendly hand on her shoulder. The pain that showed on his face was deep and sincere. "I'm terribly sorry about what she did, ma'am. About what Rachel did to Rick. But he went crazy. Killing wasn't the answer. Vengeance wasn't the answer."

Granny seemed not to have heard Carl. Trying to get control of her breathing, she said, "It-it's not that woman who killed my grandson." Her chest tightened and sobs shook her.

Carl and Luke stared at her. Carl asked, "What do you mean?"

Soft tears continued to wet Granny's cheeks. "It's ... it's the damned ..." She swallowed, seemed almost to gulp at the air. "It's the damned system that killed my Rick. My gentleman. The damned system."

Luke was shaking his head. He understood why she believed that. Rick had begun as a good guy and, by a miscarriage of justice, was turned into a serial killer. Maybe Granny had a point. "Well," said Luke, "the system's not perfect, but it's all we have."

Granny glanced at Luke. A cold look crossed her face. "So, what happened to that woman?"

Carl said, "Rick threw her overboard, but—"

He hesitated, almost unwilling to go on. "But somehow she survived the deadly fall."

Granny took the news calmly. The tears stopped flowing. She was a strong woman. After all, over the years she had lived through any crisis that fate threw at her. She said, "And even the sharks didn't want her?"


The End

# Coming Soon

## *Cruisin' With the Player*

RELISH THE CRUISE OF a lifetime as Josh boards his first cruise ship as a slot technician. His masculine perspective of life on board is bold and in-depth. Readers will find it mesmerizing, humorous, sensuous, and informative. Those who have never been on a ship will embark on the cruise of a lifetime without ever leaving the shore.

Ten percent of the profits from this book will go to charity.

Correspondence for the author should be e-mailed to: Insure411@aol. com.